Close to Home
Carolyne Aarsen

D0958282

Steeple
Hill®

Published by Steeple Hill Books™

STEEPLE HILL BOOKS

Steeple
Hill®

ISBN-13: 978-0-373-87561-0

CLOSE TO HOME

www.SteepleHill.com

Printed in U.S.A.

PLEASE RECYCLE
THIS PRODUCT IS RECYCLABLE

Recycling programs
for this product may
not exist in your area.

I said to the Lord, You are my Lord.
Apart from you I have no good thing.
—*Psalms* 16: 2

For my husband, Richard, who has always
been my strength and inspiration.

Chapter One

When the bells above the door of the coffee shop jangled, Dodie Westerveld looked up from the latte she was making and felt as if the wind had been knocked out of her.

He had returned…and with him came the dark shadows of the past.

It had been a week and a half since Jace Scholte had come back to Riverbend. And in those ten days, Dodie jumped at the sight of any man with dark hair wearing a suit. The sound of a deeply timbred voice sent her heart into overdrive.

But each jolt had been a false alarm.

Dodie knew it was just a matter of time before Jace made an appearance, however.

And the time was now.

From where she stood Dodie could see his sculpted cheekbones. A distinctive scar down one side of his face added a sense of mystique to his strong features. His icy blue eyes were edged with dark lashes.

Jace's suit sat easily on his broad shoulders. His tie was

cinched in proper lawyer fashion and he carried an expensive-looking briefcase.

Dodie swallowed, wishing she could have prepared better for this moment.

She forced her gaze back to the espresso machine, trying to contain her chaotic thoughts. Why did Janie have to choose this time to do inventory at the back of the store? Dodie could have used her sister's support.

Then, to her relief, her mother came bustling into the shop. "Hello, Dodie. Jace." She nodded in acknowledgment of each of them, her smile growing extrabright when she saw Jace.

Her mom had always liked Jace.

"Good afternoon, Mom. What can I get for you?" Dodie pasted on her brightest smile and zeroed in on her mother, who was easier to face than Jace.

"I'll have my usual, Dorothea," her mother said, glancing from Jace to Dodie, as if checking out their reaction to each other.

"Cappuccino it is," Dodie said cheerfully, bracing herself as she turned to Jace.

He was a potent reminder of what could have been. A reminder of happier times when they had dated through high school, college and that first year and a half of law school.

A reminder of her life before…

The shadows from the past loomed once again, overwhelming her for a moment.

Dodie clenched her fists and willed the darkness away. She could deal with this. It had been six years. Their life together was over. Done with.

She took another breath, relieved that the shaking in her hands subsided, that the thudding in her chest had settled to a steady beat.

"What would you like, Jace?" she asked, keeping her tone light. "Your usual?" She flashed him what she hoped was a casual smile.

The comment was a poor attempt at a joke. Since Jace had come back he hadn't been in the coffee shop once. She had wanted it to stay that way, but now that was just wishful thinking.

"Just a coffee to stay." He held her gaze, as if trying to figure her out. Dodie was the first to break the connection.

She filled a paper cup, snapped a lid on it and handed it to Jace.

"Is this a hint?" Jace asked wryly, as he took the cup.

"I believe he wanted his coffee to stay," Tilly reminded her daughter.

A flush crept up Dodie's neck and she pushed it away. Jace didn't need to see the effect he had on her this time around. A year and a half had passed since the last time he was in town. He had just passed the bar and started working at the Riverbend branch of Carson MacGregor's legal empire. Dodie managed to avoid him by finding work out of town for most of the time he'd been here. Then Jace moved back south to Edmonton, up the career ladder and out of her life again.

But two weeks ago Jace had unexpectedly returned. Rumor about town had it that he was here to clean up the mess left behind by the last lawyer working Carson MacGregor's Riverbend office.

"Sorry. I'll get you a mug," she said, holding her hand out for the cup.

"No…this is fine." Jace glanced around the coffee shop. "So this is where you're working today?" He lifted one eyebrow in her direction. Had she imagined his slight emphasis on his last word?

"Yeah. Tomorrow I'm selling eggs at the farmer's market. Monday afternoon I'm back to the thrift store. I keep busy." His question made her feel defensive. She knew her daily work schedule was vastly different from the one she would have led, had she'd stayed the course she and Jace had once mapped out for their lives when they were college sweethearts.

Their plan had been to finish law school, article for Carson MacGregor, and then, when they were both accepted to the bar, a fulfilling career of being defenders of justice and truth.

Some defender, Dodie thought. She couldn't even protect herself.

Dodie pushed down a wave of old too-familiar grief and pain. It was all Jace's fault. Being around him resurrected the agonizing memories. She should have followed her first instinct and stayed away until he returned to Edmonton. Except that would have meant running away again. And she was tired of doing that.

"Is there a day you don't work?" Jace asked.

"Sunday."

"Day of rest. Like you used to tell me," he said quietly. "Day to attend church."

Don't read more into the comment than necessary, Dodie reminded herself. You don't have to make excuses for your choices or the fact that you don't go to church as much as you used to.

"So I imagine I'll be seeing you at the meeting tonight, Dodie?" Tilly asked, as she took her cup from her daughter.

Dodie's mind skipped frantically backward, mining her memories for even a hint of which meeting her mother was referring to.

"You've forgotten, Dorothea. Haven't you?" Tilly's

disappointed sigh cleaved the air. "After promising me you would come? If you'd come regularly to church, you would have read the notice on the bulletin reminding everyone. She turned to Jace. "I swear this girl would lose her head if it wasn't so firmly attached to her neck."

Another sigh as she turned back to her daughter. "Tonight is the second meeting for the fundraiser for the Crisis Counseling Center. You said you were coming to the first one and you missed it." Tilly cupped her hands around the mug she still held, angling her head to one side in question. Not a hair on her perfectly coiffed head moved. "You do owe me." Her faintly arched brow underlined the simple statement, reminding Dodie of how grateful she'd been when her parents helped her move to her new apartment.

Dodie remembered too well how she had told her mother that if she ever needed anything to just ask. But that had been three months ago, and she assumed her mother had simply taken her promise as another way of saying thank-you.

Apparently she'd been wrong.

"I'm sorry. I forgot." Dodie reached up to push a stray strand of her own blond hair back behind her ear, then stopped, trying not to fidget. She noticed Jace discreetly sitting down at a table, ostensibly to give mother and daughter some much-needed privacy.

"You can make up for last time. I asked Randy Webber, the chairman of the fundraiser, if you could still come and he said yes." Tilly glanced past Dodie and smiled. "There you are, Janie. I had wondered where you'd gone. Maybe you can help me convince Dorothea to live up to her obligations and help out with the fundraiser?"

"Is that the one for the Crisis Center?" Janie asked,

tossing a towel over her shoulder. She adjusted the bandanna holding back her dark hair as she gave Jace a piercing glance.

"That's the one."

"But…" Janie glanced from her mother to Dodie. "You can't go to that fundraiser, anyway."

Dodie felt a flush of relief. Janie was going to come up with an excuse for her. That's what sisters were for!

"That's Dodie's birthday," Janie explained.

Tilly lifted one perfectly plucked brow. "And?"

Janie sighed. "I was going to have a party. It's her thirtieth, remember?"

Dodie sighed, wishing her sister would forget.

Many years ago, she hadn't imagined that on her thirtieth birthday she would be a single woman flitting from job to job, still unable to settle down with either a man or a career.

Her vision, at that time, included the beginning of a promising career as a lawyer.

And a somewhat hazier vision included being married to the man standing across the counter from her.

"But I'll be attending the fundraiser, as will your father," Tilly protested. "Surely you can have her party on another day?"

"We always have the thirtieth birthday parties right on the day. Tradition," Janie said, angling her sister a triumphant look.

Dodie glanced from her sister to her mother, dread settling into the pit of her stomach.

Caught between a rock and a hard place. Commit to the fundraiser and end up working with her mother, or commit to the birthday party and spend the night being confronted with the stark reality of her life.

"Sure. I'll help," she said with a false heartiness. "What time is the meeting?"

"Six-thirty. Tonight."

"Okay. I'll be there." Not willingly, but she had no other choice.

"That's wonderful. I've got Jace to join, as well."

Jace? On the committee? She had just made a huge tactical error.

Her mother's eyes narrowed slightly, as if she could read Dodie's mind. "So I'll see you tonight, then."

"Yeah. Sure." She gave her mother a wan smile, let her gaze tick quickly over Jace, then ducked her head to put the money they had given her in the cash register.

Tilly joined Jace at the table in the corner. Dodie turned her back on them, fighting the urge to bang her head on the counter. What had she done? There was no way she could work with Jace.

Janie sidled up to her and nudged her with her elbow. "I gave you an out," she hissed. "Why didn't you take it?"

"I told you I don't want a birthday party." Dodie glanced over her shoulder, but her mother and Jace were still deep in conversation.

"And helping Mom and Jace with a fundraiser is a better option?"

Dodie pulled her attention back to her sister, but she couldn't answer Janie's question. Janie knew how hard Dodie had tried to avoid Jace Scholte the last time he was in town. Which suited Janie fine. She had never liked Jace and hadn't been too disappointed when Dodie had come back from her spur-of-the moment trip to Europe, six years ago, claiming she and Jace were over.

"Look, I owe Mom," Dodie said with a heavy sigh. "And I said I would come. So I'll make an appearance, find out what's up and see if there's some way I can be involved without actually attending the meetings."

"So we can still have your birthday party?"

"Well, no. If I'm involved in the fundraiser, then I'll have to show up at that, won't I?" Dodie gave her sister a tight smile, then went to the back of the shop to get some more coffee beans as she tried to untangle the mess she'd just gotten in.

You said you would, an annoying voice reminded her. *And what would your mother think if you tried to get out of it? Or Jace, for that matter?*

But I don't need to prove anything, she countered. Either to my mother or to Jace.

Sure, she used to be Miss Involvement. Sure, she used to be on the school's honor roll, help at every single church function, go to Bible Study and have regular devotions.

What did all that busywork get her?

Zip. Less than zip, in fact.

She stopped her thoughts from making a nasty detour into the past. She had to focus on finding a way to keep her mother happy and herself away from Jace and all the memories he dredged up from the past.

By the time Dodie was finished in the back of the coffee shop, Jace and Tilly were gone, and she felt as if she could breathe again.

For the rest of the day, she poured coffee, sold muffins and cookies, traded cheerful banter with the patrons and with each passing minute tried to find a solution to her problem.

Surely she could find another way to repay her mother and keep Janie from throwing her an unwanted birthday party?

By the time she and Janie locked up for the day, she

had found a partial solution to her problem: she wouldn't go tonight—simple as that. If Jace would be there then she just had to stay away. No sense resurrecting the past. Besides, he was only in town temporarily. He would be gone again, just like last time.

Although she felt a pang of guilt about letting her mother down again, she didn't see any other option. Hopefully, she'd find a way to get Tilly to understand her side of things.

Her mind made up, she planned on phoning her mother after the meeting to ask her what job she could do that wouldn't necessitate attending the meetings.

Dodie was mopping up when a knock on the locked shop door caught her attention.

Stifling a groan, Janie wiped her hands on the cloth and tossed it in the sink. "Now what?" she mumbled to herself, as she opened the door for her mother.

"Are you girls just about done?" Tilly asked, as Janie let her in.

"We were just cleaning up," Janie said.

"I'm so glad I caught you here." Tilly's voice was bright. Cheerful even. "This works out perfectly."

Dodie turned, dread hanging over her like a cloud. "What do you mean?"

"I need a ride to the meeting," Tilly explained. Her manicured fingertips adjusted the lapels of her blazer. "I had to unexpectedly drop my car off at the mechanic, and I won't be able to pick it up until tomorrow."

Dodie sensed what was coming next.

"So we can go together to the meeting, right?" Tilly emphasized her suggestion with a lift of one perfectly plucked eyebrow.

Dodie should have known she couldn't buck her

mother. Tilly Westerveld could teach courses on manipulation and get even the most reluctant person to do her bidding.

Fine, Dodie thought. She'd go to this meeting and *only* this meeting.

Tilly pointed at Dodie's ripped blue jeans and hot pink T-shirt. "You should go home and change first."

Dodie lifted her shoulders in a vague shrug. "I don't mind wearing this tonight." If her mother was going to finagle her into making sure she attended, then she had to take her as she was.

Tilly's glare almost sent Dodie's hair flying back. "Very well, then, let's go."

In that moment Dodie felt every bit of the disappointment she had subjected her family to since she dropped out of law school six years ago.

She grabbed her denim jacket and her purse. "Okay. I'm ready."

The only expression on her mother's face was a faint tightening around her lips as Dodie wound a long, purple scarf around her neck. But then she forced a smile, waved at Janie and marched out of the coffee shop ahead of her daughter.

Dodie hadn't prayed in years, but she came perilously close to it as she fished in her oversize purse for her car keys. Just get through this meeting, she reminded herself during the short drive to Riverbend Hall. Make the right noises and stay as far away from Jace as possible. Then find a way to get out of any further meetings.

"What are you plotting?" Tilly demanded.

Dodie stopped at the traffic light and shot her mother a shocked glance. How did she know? "Nothing."

"Who are you kidding? You've got your lips pursed, and you only do that when you're planning something."

Dodie focused intently on the road as the light turned green. "Just thinking about the fundraiser meeting."

"If you say so…" Tilly's eyes suddenly lit up. "Though I know Jace is only working here long enough to help out Carson MacGregor, I'm so pleased to see him involved in the community. He's such a good person." She shrugged. "I was surprised the two of you didn't have more to talk about today."

"What's to talk about?" Dodie replied, turning onto the street where the Riverbend Hall was located.

"Dodie, the two of you were thick as thieves. Your father and I were so pleased." Tilly paused a moment, as if to make sure Dodie was well aware of how suitable her mother thought Jace was for her. "In fact, we suspected wedding bells—"

"So, tell me, how thick are thieves?" Dodie interrupted her mother's meanderings. "Is the comment referring to their intelligence? Or their girth? And if so, why thick as opposed to thin? I mean—"

Tilly lifted her hand. "Don't bother with your silly comments. I know you don't want me talking about Jace and for some inane reason you aren't interested in him anymore." She sighed. "Though I can't see why not. He's as good-looking as he ever was, and that scar he got from the car accident actually accentuates his looks. And let's not forget that he's a successful lawyer with a bright future ahead of him…"

Dodie wanted to make a smart remark about the places Jace was going, but she realized any reaction to her mother's litany of Jace's attributes, negative or positive, would only encourage her to keep prattling on.

"Here we are," Dodie said with a forced note of brightness in her voice. She parked the car in the empty parking lot by the hall. "First ones here."

"No, we are not. I saw a few cars parked at the side of the hall," her mother said when she got out of the car. "I'm sure one of them was Jace's."

Dodie flipped her purse over her shoulder and wrapped her arms around her middle as she strode across the parking lot. Enough about Jace already, she thought, jogging up the steps to the hall. She just wanted to get this over with!

The echoing screech of the door announced their arrival. Dodie walked in behind her mother, glancing around the room.

A few people sat near the back. One girl looked back and gave Tilly a quick wave of recognition. Jace, standing by a table at the front of the room, looked up, as well. The smile on his face shifted as he caught Dodie's eye.

Well, she wasn't crazy about being here, either, she fumed, plunking herself down in the nearest chair at the back of the room.

Her mother joined Jace at the front of the room.

While they chatted, Dodie crossed her arms and pretended to be interested in the bits of crepe paper clinging to the walls, left over from the last wedding held here.

She'd celebrated enough of her cousins' weddings in this very hall, she thought with a touch of melancholy. Sarah and Logan's, Ethan and Hannah's… And she fondly recalled the love that had filled this very room during her sister Janie's second marriage to Luke.

As a young girl dreams of her own wedding had gone through various iterations, but the one constant had been a big, family-filled celebration here, at the Riverbend Hall.

Six years ago the vague plans had included lilies in tall,

crystal vases, twined with ivy and surrounded by small votives at their bases, sage-green napkins with silver napkin rings on creamy damask tablecloths and bags of homemade cookies for favors.

For a time, she even had a groom in the picture. Tall, dark, handsome, with an intriguing scar down his one cheek.

Dodie wrenched herself back from the bittersweet memories. She closed her eyes and tried to center herself in the now.

"Dorothea, come here, honey." Her mother's quiet voice broke into Dodie's ineffectual self-talk. Though her mother hadn't raised her voice, the inherent demand in it was hard to ignore.

So Dodie got up and joined Tilly, who was holding a piece of paper.

"Because you missed the first meeting the committees have been established already," Tilly said.

Dodie kept her attention on the paper in her mother's hand, trying unsuccessfully to ignore Jace.

He still wore his suit, the striped silk tie still cinched around his startling white shirt. Typical lawyer dress, she thought. And far removed from the scruffy blue jeans and T-shirts he favored throughout high school, college and law school.

His gaze flicked over her and returned to Tilly.

Dodie didn't know if she should feel insulted at his off-hand treatment of her, then decided she didn't care. She tucked her hands inside the front pockets of her jeans.

"Which one would you like to join?" her mother was asking.

Dodie pulled herself back to the present with a start. "I don't want to be on a committee," she said, glancing down the lists.

"Why not?" her mother asked.

Because I'm not coming to any more of these meetings and committees meant ongoing commitments and more meetings, she thought.

"I like something I can do on my own time. I'm too busy for meetings." She made the mistake of looking directly at Jace and catching the disappointment in his eyes. It shouldn't have bothered her, but it did. At one time his opinion meant everything to her.

She blinked and broke eye contact.

Don't get pulled in, she told herself. Don't cave. Once he's done his work here, he'll be gone again.

"Why don't you have a look at the list?" Tilly suggested. "You might see something you can help with."

To satisfy her mother, Dodie took the paper and found a committee she could probably help on.

"Do you have a pen, Mom?" she asked, laying the paper down so she could write on it.

But a masculine hand appeared in her vision. Without looking up, Dodie plucked the pen out of Jace's fingers, trying not to notice how the metal was still warm from his hand.

She scribbled her name under the committee responsible for gathering donations for the silent auction, then set the pen on the table.

Phoning from home, that she could do. Simple and straightforward. Work through the list and she was done.

"That's one of the more critical committees," Jace said, as he picked up his pen. He lifted an eyebrow in her direction.

Dodie shrugged his concern away. "I think I can handle it."

"Think?" His eyes seemed to hold a challenge.

Dodie didn't look away. "Know," she replied.

"Okay. We'll be getting together tomorrow night to put together a list of potential donors from various towns."

"We?" Dodie frowned.

"Yeah. I'm on the same committee." Jace took his pen and pointed to his name scrawled at the top of the list.

How could she have missed it?

"Our first meeting will be here," he said.

"I'm in Mayerthorpe for farmer's market, but I'll be back in time," she said, holding his gaze.

"Good."

"Well, I'm glad that's settled," Tilly said, patting her daughter on the shoulder. "Jace has some more information on the fundraiser printed out here. Why don't you read the material while we wait for the meeting to start?"

She handed Dodie a cardboard folder.

As Dodie flipped through the material, she couldn't help but be impressed with how organized it all was. In one inside pocket was a list of all the committee members. In the other, a description of the purpose of the fundraiser.

She sat down and started reading. Though she knew very well what the fundraiser was for, she made sure to read every word on every piece of paper in the entire brochure. That way she didn't have to pay attention to Jace, hovering at the front of the room.

The money would fund a building to house a Crisis Counseling Center. The center had a few people on staff in an office sharing space with a local dentist. They needed to expand their services and in order to do that, were desperate for a new building. Hence the fundraiser.

Dodie traced her finger over the artist's rendering of the building, with its Victorian-brick facade. At one time she had made plans to work at the center.

To that end she had taken correspondence courses, building on her college degree. But she hadn't found the time or the motivation to finish the course.

Maybe. One day.

She looked up again and caught Jace looking at her. A sense of foreboding held her in its grip.

Working with Jace was a bad idea in so many ways.

What if all the memories she had shoved deep down came roaring back?

She'd just have to make sure she did everything within her power to keep that from happening.

Chapter Two

He shouldn't have been surprised that Dodie hadn't shown up to the meeting.

Even though the other committee member had left fifteen minutes ago, Jace had stayed around the hall in the faint hope that Dodie would come rushing in full of apologies and excuses. He'd been willing to give her the benefit of the doubt but it had all been for naught.

Sighing, Jace glanced at his watch again and gathered his papers. It was time to go home and get caught up on work. Dodie was a no-show.

He shouldn't have been surprised, but he couldn't help but feel disappointed. When he agreed to come back to his hometown of Riverbend it was with the vague hope that he could have one more chance to find out why his old girlfriend had changed so much.

Obviously he wasn't going to find anything out tonight.

In spite of his irritation with Dodie, he had to smile as he drove through the tree-lined streets of Riverbend. He never thought that he'd one day see familiar landmarks that he'd always walked past—the hardware store, the post office, the movie theater, his old high school—through the windshield of a silver BMW.

How things change, he mused, wincing when his thoughts immediately drifted back to Dodie again.

And why did his mind immediately slip back to Dodie again?

Why couldn't he get her off his mind? He wished he could just treat her as casually as he treated any of the old friends who had stayed behind in Riverbend.

He had managed to avoid running into her for two weeks. But when Tilly asked to talk to him at the coffee shop, he knew that seeing his old girlfriend was inevitable.

Old girlfriend.

The words conjured up too many painful memories of him and Dodie, walking hand in hand down these same streets. First as high school sweethearts, then as college students returning home to work, save up money and head back to the city once again.

Forcing thoughts of Dodie out of his mind, he pulled up to his old house, grabbed his briefcase and got out of the car.

Spring was definitely in the air. He took a moment to let the scent of the new season wash over him. The row of Mayday trees he and his father had planted many years ago, were in full bloom, sending out the heady scent of almonds. The trees arching over the street held the tender green of new growth.

I missed this, he thought, looking around his old neighborhood.

He wished his mother still lived here, but after his father died four years ago, she began talking about moving to Ontario, where her own sister lived. A year ago she'd made up her mind and moved.

Leaving the house to Jace's care.

His only other family was a sister who'd answered the call to do mission work in Nigeria.

Only a couple of friends still lived in Riverbend. So other than Carson's promise of a promotion if he came back here to clean up the mess the previous lawyer had left behind, precious little called him back to Riverbend.

And Dodie?

Jace banished the question. She had taken up enough of his thoughts. Besides, he was tired of seeing her wasting her potential working away at jobs that were a waste of her talent.

He strode up the sidewalk to his house. Once inside, he went to the bedroom off the living room. His old bedroom, now his temporary office. A few darker rectangles marked places where posters had once lined the walls.

If he closed his eyes, he could hear the strains of the country music his sister always insisted on playing, coming down the hallway.

And he could hear his parents arguing in the kitchen, going over the usual ground—the constant shortage of money and how they were going to manage.

His glance took in the peeling paint on the walls, the bare lightbulb suspended from the ceiling. Though it was his childhood home, it always represented his parents' struggle to make a living. Ever since his father's disabling accident at the mill where he worked, things had been difficult financially. His mother worked at the local grocery store to augment the meager disability check his father got.

As long as Jace could remember, money had been a problem. That was why he became a lawyer—so money would not be a worry in his life.

He threw his briefcase on the desk just as the phone rang.

He picked it up and glanced at the clock. Habit. Got to make sure you catch any billable hour you can, he thought.

"So how are things down in the boondocks?" Chuck MacGregor's overly hearty voice called out over the phone line.

"Can't believe one guy could do so much in only two years at this office," Jace said. He tucked the phone under his ear as he picked up one of the files he'd brought home to work on.

"That's why Dad got you to go out there. You're the man for the job," Chuck said. "Glad I could stay back here and keep working my own files."

Jace repressed his sigh. Being the boss's son was probably the bigger reason Carson MacGregor didn't ask Chuck to come and do this.

But no matter. Anything that put Jace in Carson's good graces would be an advancement for him.

"You connected with any of the old school buds yet?" Chuck asked.

"Not many of them around. Most of them did what I did—left."

"Smart people. I heard Dodie was still around? How's she doing?"

"Same as before. Wasting her time." And potential. During high school, during his wild years before he wised up, Dodie had been the one who challenged him to do more. Now, thanks to her, he was where he was.

Why she was where she was would remain a mystery.

"That's too bad. She had brainpower. She married yet?"

"Nope."

"So you still have a chance?" Chuck said with an edge of sarcasm.

"What can I do for you Chuck?" Jace asked, ignoring

Chuck's question. He didn't want to let old feelings about Dodie superimpose themselves on the present.

"I'm working on the Henderson file…"

Jace felt a shiver of apprehension trickle down his spine. Chuck had been his friend since third grade, when Jace had rescued him from a playground bully. Jace had gotten a bloody nose out of the deal, as well as Chuck's eternal friendship. They stayed close all through junior and senior high. In college they roomed together, and when Dodie left it was Chuck who consoled him, Chuck who told him that Dodie had always considered herself a cut above them both.

In spite of that, Jace was very aware of his friend's true nature. He had seen firsthand how Chuck always took care of Chuck.

"You're not poaching my clients, are you?" Jace asked, trying to sound as if he was joking, though he wasn't.

"Too busy for that," Chuck said with a laugh. "Dad asked me to have a look at the buy-out clause."

And soon they were immersed in legalese and work.

When they were done Jace glanced at the clock. Nine-thirty, and they were both still working.

But that was how one got ahead. And getting ahead was what Jace wanted right now. Especially after growing up surrounded by poverty.

He looked around his room, a grim reminder of the discrepancies between his and Chuck's lives. How often had he come back here after spending time at the palatial MacGregor's place and wished for more?

And when Chuck moved to Edmonton, his parents sold their house and bought an even bigger one in Edmonton. And Chuck's father, Carson MacGregor, started an even bigger legal practice, leaving the one in Riverbend in the hands of his partner.

The MacGregors always had so much more than the Scholtes.

And now Jace was on his way to that elusive "more." If he did his job here, who knew what could happen? Who knew what kind of place he could build for himself?

But whom would he share it with?

Jace let the question linger a moment. Scrambling up the legal ladder didn't leave much time for romance. He'd had a few girlfriends, but none of them took, as Chuck would say.

None of them compared to the girl who had once held his heart.

He let an image of Dodie linger, comparing her to the girl he used to date. Dodie-of-now had a faded pink streak in her hair, wore clothes that could only be described as eclectic. Short skirts, high boots, oversize dangling earrings all in unusual shades of pink, turquoise and purple. She seemed to be deliberate about cultivating an image far removed from the girl who wore plain blue jeans and button-down blouses.

The girl Jace had been captivated with.

Jace glanced over at the bookshelf and, on a whim, pulled out his high school yearbook. Dust caked its spine.

The picture it fell open to took up half the page. Dodie Westerveld, her long blond hair flowing over her shoulders, her hands raised above her head in a gesture of victory. The photo was a study in uncontrolled exuberance and carefree joy. A picture of Dodie.

Before.

Jace sighed as he flipped through the book to another familiar page. Dodie's single picture with her signature scrawled in sensible blue ink.

"To Jace, make sure you're headed in the right direction and I'll be there beside you."

Back then Dodie was an honor student who was president of the high school student body, a strong leader in the church's youth group, outspoken about her faith and proud of her beliefs.

But the daughter of Dan Westerveld wasn't the kind of girl who would go out with just anybody, and she had made that fairly clear to Jace the first time he had asked her out. Jace liked to party with his friend, Chuck, and he liked to hang out with a questionable crowd.

But Jace wasn't that easily put off. He was definitely interested in Dodie Westerveld. But no matter how much he turned on the charm, she kept saying no.

He even went to church a couple of times to see what was up, but still no luck with Dodie.

However, going to church had shown him other possibilities, had given him other things to think about. Had made him ponder eternity and where he was heading.

Then came the night Chuck MacGregor drove to Jace's place drunk and out of control. He had tried to ask a girl out and she turned him down. He was angry and he shouldn't have been driving.

Jace forcibly took the keys away from him to drive him home. As they were driving, Chuck tried to grab the wheel, wrenching it out of Jace's hands.

Jace could so clearly recall the sound of the tires squealing, glass breaking, the crunch of metal hitting the ground and the feeling of the entire weight of the vehicle tumbling slowly, end over end.

When it came to a stop, Chuck was pinned inside the burning car, unconscious. Jace had been thrown free.

He had run back to the car, scrambled inside, cutting

his face in the process—yet still managed to pull his friend to safety before the car blew up.

Jace unconsciously fingered the scar on his face, remembering all too well the fear that had paralyzed him as he saw Chuck inside the burning car. The sheer panic as he tried to pull his friend free, and the terror when he realized how close the two of them had come to death.

Though the accident wasn't his fault, it was a wake-up call. Jace pulled his life together, got his grades up and started attending church with his parents. He went to Bible Study and tried to keep his motives pure, but he did hope that Dodie took notice.

She did, and by the time prom rolled around, he worked up enough nerve to ask her. No one was more surprised than he was when she accepted…and at the end of a fun-filled night, he knew she was the one he wanted.

Their life was on the same course when they headed to college. He decided to emulate his mentor, Carson MacGregor, who had offered to help pay for his schooling in gratitude for what Jace had done for Chuck. Carson had also offered both him and Dodie a position in his law firm when they were done with their education.

Life was good. He and Dodie had dreams and plans.

And then, one day, completely out of the blue, Dodie abandoned her apartment, left Edmonton and Jace. No note, no phone call, no e-mail. Nothing.

He panicked. Phoned around.

He found out from her family that she had unexpectedly gone backpacking in Europe. That they weren't sure when she was going to be back. And no, they didn't know what happened, either, if indeed anything had happened.

She never came back to Edmonton. Never came back to school and never, in all the years since, contacted him…

Just forget about her, he reprimanded himself sharply as he shook off the unsettling memories. Picking up the next file, he buried himself in his work and vowed to keep his mind on the here and now.

You don't need to be here, she thought. You don't need to prove anything.

Dodie hugged her purse close as she stood on the sidewalk in front of Jace's old house, trying to psych herself up for the meeting he had called.

He'd left a message on her cell phone Saturday night, asking her where she'd been and telling her that there was a new meeting called for Wednesday night.

All the way here tonight she'd gone over her excuses for missing the meeting on Saturday.

Wasn't her fault her car quit. Wasn't her fault her cell phone had no coverage where she was stranded. Wasn't her fault she had to walk back to Mayerthorpe to get someone to help her get her car going again. And it wasn't her fault that by the time she got everything going again, the sun had long set and the meeting was long over.

But the excuses sounded feeble, even to her ears.

She clutched the straps of her purse and stared at the house she had come to from time to time in high school. A pale green misted the leaves of the trees hanging over the street. The prized peonies that Jace's mom loved were a mass of green in the front of the house. Some already sported fat, tight buds.

Spring was making itself known.

Come summer Jace would be gone. Back to the city and back out of her life.

If she turned and walked down the sidewalk, she could avoid him again. That would be the wisest plan of action.

Jace belonged in the past. Getting involved with him in any way, shape or form was dangerous and costly.

Mom will find out if you don't go, the little voice said.

Well, so what? She'd disappointed her mother many times in the past few years, what was one more disappointment to add to the pile?

You owe her.

Dodie sighed, trying to imagine the repercussions of skipping out on this obligation.

That would mean missing the fundraiser. Which would free up that night, which in turn would give her sister carte blanche to plan a birthday party she simply couldn't face.

Thank goodness she wasn't the only one here, Dodie thought, glancing at the silver BMW and the old truck parked in front of the house.

She couldn't help but wonder who they belonged to. She couldn't imagine Jace driving a fancy Beemer, but she doubted he drove the rusted-out old truck.

At least it wouldn't be the two of them, she thought, marching up the sidewalk and knocking on the door.

The door opened and Dodie couldn't stop the jolt of familiarity.

Jace wore faded blue jeans and a worn cotton shirt. More surprising, his feet were bare.

A memory wafted into the present. Jace sitting on the grass on the college campus, kicking off his shoes, then releasing a sigh as he dug his feet into the grass. He used to hate wearing shoes and wore sandals well into fall, at least until his toes turned purple from the cold.

She had always teased him that when he became a lawyer, he would have to smarten up and buy a suit. With shoes.

When they started law school, he did. And he began

to transform into the lawyer that would make Carson MacGregor proud.

Dodie pulled her oversize purse close against her as she stifled the memory.

His glance skimmed over her. "I'm glad you could make it this time," he said.

She resisted the urge to explain.

He looked over her shoulder. "You walked here?"

"My car is currently decorating the lot at Wierenga Motors."

"Broken down?"

"As of this Saturday, yes." And that was all the explanation she was going to give him. "So, shall we get started?"

He just held her gaze, his own expression serious. For a heartbeat she wondered what was going on behind those enigmatic eyes. "I set everything up in the kitchen," he said, turning back inside.

As she followed him through the house, Dodie's gaze flicked over the living room, taking in the few pieces of old, worn furniture—left over from his mother—and nothing else.

The kitchen was as austere as the living room, holding only a wooden table-and-chair set. Nothing on the counters and nothing on the walls.

It looked temporary and unwelcoming.

Jace pulled out a chair for each of them, and Dodie frowned. "Just the two of us?" she asked, as she unwound the green-and-blue scarf from around her neck.

"Sheila Kippers was supposed to come, but she had a family emergency. Her daughter fell and broke her arm."

Dodie frowned and poked her thumb over her shoulder. "That fancy car out front…?"

"Is mine." Jace looked as defensive as she had felt and

Dodie was surprised. Both at his reaction and at the vehicle. She knew Jace wanted more in his life; she just never thought it would involve a luxury vehicle that cost almost as much as the house they were in right now.

"But the truck?"

"My dad's."

"I was sorry to hear about his death," Dodie said quietly.

"Were you?" He threw the question out lightly, but it hit Dodie hard.

Back in the day, Dodie had gotten to know his father. She knew that Jace, his only son, was his pride and joy and that he'd pinned a lot of expectations on Jace's success. Nevertheless, she'd been impressed with his warmth and obvious love for his son.

"I *am* sorry," Dodie reiterated.

Jace held her gaze for an extra beat. "Like I said, it's been a while."

Dodie swallowed, looking away. Time to change the subject. "And how is your mom doing in Ontario?"

"She's good." Jace gave her a polite smile. "Do you want anything to drink?"

Dodie waved off his request. The sooner they could get started, the sooner they would be finished and the sooner she could be away from his unsettling presence. Maybe with time she could get used to him. Maybe she could get to the point that seeing him wouldn't send her emotions into a tailspin. For now, however, she had to keep her guard up.

"Okay, then let's get started. If you don't mind, I'd like to get through this stuff quickly. I've still got a ton of work to do tonight."

"Working after hours?" Dodie asked, as she pulled a pen and notepad out of her purse.

"For a lawyer there is no nine-to-five."

"Especially if you're working for Carson MacGregor." Dodie didn't mean for the sharp tone to edge her voice, but it was already out there, and Jace was already lifting his one eyebrow.

"Carson is a fair and generous man. He's been good to me and Chuck."

Dodie snatched up the paper Jace had laid on the table, more than ready to move on. "So, what's your plan of attack on this?"

Dodie waited for him to reply and when he didn't, she looked up at him.

His face was so familiar and yet not. The years had made the scar on the side of his face more pronounced, had etched new lines around his eyes.

And hovering, in the depths of his blue eyes, she saw a question she couldn't acknowledge. She felt her heart lurch as she intrinsically knew what he was going to ask.

She couldn't delve into the past, couldn't relive what she had worked so hard to put behind her.

"I'm guessing you want to divide the list up," she said, dropping her gaze to the papers in front of her, determined to move on.

"That was the plan."

"Great…a lawyer with a plan. I feel like I should be afraid." Dodie kept her tone casual. This was the only way she was going to get through this.

Jace was quiet and Dodie pushed on. "So, this is the master sheet we're working from?"

"Yes. My secretary drew it up."

The paper held an alphabetized list of all the businesses in Riverbend, Preston and Kolvik, and their phone numbers. "So what do you figure, split this up and see how far we get?" Dodie asked, matching Jace's businesslike tone. As long as things proceeded this way, she could handle this.

"I should stipulate that we'd like more than the usual travel mugs and T-shirts, if possible. I want to make this fundraiser impressive, get some really unique items. Apparently the committee has been working on this for a while now. They've already booked a very dynamic speaker. We've reserved the arena in town, and in order to fill it, we need something special to draw a good crowd."

"The people of Riverbend are generous. Shouldn't be too hard," Dodie said.

He handed her a copy of the sheet. "Are you sure you're up to this?"

"I came to this meeting, didn't I?" Dodie said, shifting through the other papers, trying to keep her voice neutral.

His silence seemed to imply something else, and Dodie shook her head in mock consternation. "Jace, where's the trust? Where's the love?" She flashed him a quick smile, fighting to maintain an air of joviality.

"This isn't just a lark for me. I need to make this fundraiser work."

"Why is this important to you? You couldn't get away from Riverbend fast enough. You've never really been attached to this place. Why bother getting involved now?" Dodie tamped down her irritation as she drew in a long, slow breath. She knew she shouldn't get into a sparring match with him. She needed to keep her emotions under control.

Jace sighed, then leaned back in his chair. "Let's just say that I've got a lot riding on this event."

"Like a promotion?"

Jace shrugged. "No secret there. I will do what I can for Carson and the company. And anything I do that reflects well on me reflects well on the law firm."

"Old Man MacGregor must adore you." She shouldn't have let that note of scorn slip into her voice. She was moving into dangerous territory.

"We get along well."

"I'm sure part of your devotion has to do with the accident you and Chuck were in." No sooner had the snippy words left her mouth than she wished she could pull them back. The jab hearkened back to memories of high school. To scrapes Jace and his friend would get in and Carson would dig them out of. The most serious one being the car accident that had given Jace his scar.

And had made him turn his life around.

"I got this job strictly on my own merit." The steely tone in his voice told her she had hit a sore spot.

"I'm sorry." She kept the apology simple. She needed to keep her focus on the business at hand. "Don't worry, Jace, I'll do my best to make this fundraiser a success."

"I'd appreciate that. Like I said, I need for it to do well."

"You're ambitious these days, hmm?"

"Yeah, well, it seems we've traded places in that department."

His tone was too familiar. She had to put a stop to this little trip down memory lane.

"Things change. People change," she said with an airy wave of her hand. "I'm using my talents in my own way. And you're stuck with me and those talents."

He didn't say anything to that and, in spite of her need to keep her distance, she didn't like the idea that he thought of her as unambitious.

She lifted a brow. "I'll tell you what, Scholte. I know for

a fact I can get more dollars' worth of donations than you and Sheila combined," she said, a challenge in her voice.

"Really?" Jace crossed his arms over his chest, looking incredulous.

"Really." Dodie leaned forward, her elbows resting on the table, her body language showing more confidence than she felt.

"Getting donations is one thing, but raising a substantial amount of money is something else," Jace cautioned her.

"Good thing I am something else, as you were always so fond of saying." As soon as the words left her mouth, she felt like snatching them back. She had promised herself, before she came here, that she wasn't going to revisit their past together. They'd both changed over the years and there was no turning back.

"So you really think you can raise the most lucrative donations, Dorothea Alicia Grace Westerveld?"

His use of her full name created an unexpected tug on those old memories, like a hook pulling out what she had just pushed down.

She pressed her hand against her chest, holding back the thundering of her heart.

Don't go there, she told herself. Don't go back.

"Yeah. I do," she said, throwing the challenge back with forced bravado, trying to counteract the feelings he was bringing to the forefront.

"Very well, I'm proposing a little contest. If you get better donations than me, I have to take you out for dinner. If I get more than you, then you have to take me out for dinner."

What kind of a contest was that?

"To the winner's choice of restaurant," Jace added.

Dodie hesitated. She was fairly sure she would win. She knew most of the people in this town better than Jace did.

"Scared?" Jace taunted.

"No. I just think it's silly."

"Then…" He lifted one hand in a languid gesture.

"Okay. I accept. Dinner at any place I choose."

"You're that sure you're going to win?"

Dodie glanced down at the papers and gave a decisive nod, more to assure herself than him. "Oh yeah. I'm that sure."

"And you're here for the long haul?"

A casual observer wouldn't have caught the faint edge in Jace's voice or been able to interpret the subtext inherent in his words.

"Of course I am." She couldn't stop the hurt from creeping into her voice.

His eyes softened and for a moment she thought he was going to touch her. She stepped away.

"You've let me know how important this is to you. I wouldn't want to get in the way of your ambitions."

"You make ambition sound like a dirty word."

"You didn't used to care about that."

"Well, people change. As you said." Jace held her gaze for a heartbeat longer than he needed to. He looked like he wanted to ask her a question, like he wanted to shift the conversation back to that precarious moment a while ago.

She held his eyes, willing herself not to look away. "I am not a quitter." She enunciated each word carefully. Just to make sure he got it.

The dubious expression on his face created a question and stoked her anger; a far preferable emotion than the other feelings hovering between her and Jace. "Unlike you," she said, drawing on her anger, "I know this town. I don't just come hopping back in and out when it suits me. You can doubt my ability to stick things through to the end, but I'm not one to turn my back on the people that matter."

"Really?" His eyes narrowed now, as if trying to get past the facade she'd worked so hard to create.

Too late she realized how she had neatly been snared in her own statement.

She lowered her eyes, her hands grasping the paper as she fought to keep herself grounded in the present.

"Dodie…why are you like this?" he asked. "What happened?"

Thankfully his voice held an impatient edge. His question was easier to brush off if he was angry with her. Any hint of caring would have undone her.

She shoved her paper into the folder she had taken along, then stuffed the folder in her bag. "Anything else?" she asked, as she got up and slung her bag over her shoulder.

Their gazes caught and held, and Dodie could feel his frustration humming in the air. Then his expression grew enigmatic. "You'll keep me posted on your progress?"

"If I need any help, I'll ask." Dodie spun around and strode down the hallway and out the door.

She was halfway down the sidewalk before she unclenched her fists, before the tightness across her forehead eased away. She shouldn't have let him get to her.

She had made her own choices out of self-preservation. The only way she could get past that horrible night was by keeping the memories locked down.

And for the past few years, she had managed.

She folded her arms tight against her chest, as her mind, against her will, flashed back to that night.

The pain. The utter humiliation. How unclean she felt afterward.

The man who had violated her had taunted her, telling her that she had asked for it. When he was done, she had stumbled out of the room. Then she went home, packed her bags and ran.

Dodie breathed in and out. In and out, struggling to calm herself, to push the memories down.

No matter what happened, she could not tell Jace the real reason she had to keep him at arm's length. Keep him away from her heart.

If he found out the real reason she had left those many years ago, he would pity her.

And that she couldn't handle.

Chapter Three

"**Y**ou're married?" Dodie pulled her attention from the other vendors at the Riverbend Farmer's Market to Paul Grady, the middle-aged man standing in front of her.

Paul wore his usual plaid woolen coat and still carried the battered guitar that he used to busk at the entrance to the farmer's market.

But today he was clean-shaven and his long, thinning hair neatly combed. Even if she didn't believe what he said, she had to believe what she saw. Paul seldom shaved, and the only time she saw him with neat hair was when he was playing a gig on the folk-music circuit.

But that wasn't starting for at least a month or two.

"Yeah. Happened about a week ago." Paul sent her a wink. "It's great. You should try it."

Dodie ignored the hint, still trying to absorb the idea that Paul, the footloose gent who had been single all his life, was now married.

"So…who…?"

"Helen Lennox."

"*The* Helen Lennox?" Dodie tried to make sense of this

surprising information, sure Paul was either teasing her or had become delusional.

"Yup." Paul grinned happily. "You'll have to come up and see us sometime. She'd love some company."

Just like that. A casual invitation to meet Helen Lennox, one of Dodie's favorite singers. Don't let your mouth fall open, Dodie, she thought. "Well…sure…I guess. Are you living at…your place?"

"Yeah. She likes it up here. Says it's rustic."

Rustic was a kind description. Dodie tried to imagine Helen Lennox of the spangled guitar and sweeping formal dresses being happy in the log cabin Paul had built with his bachelor brother over the course of five years.

"I'd love to come."

"Tonight?"

"Okay." Dodie was dumbfounded. Sure, she had visited Paul before, bringing him the occasional meal, some baking and the farm-fresh eggs he enjoyed, but to come for a visit to see Helen Lennox…

"I think she's a bit lonely. Could get to know some local women. Me and the Lord are working on her to come to church. She's thinking on it. You'd like her—she's real sweet."

I'm sure I would, Dodie thought, still trying to process the information. Helen Lennox. "So how did you meet?" she asked, trying to not project her incredulity into her voice.

Paul shrugged. "I was doing a gig down at a coffee house in Calgary a year ago. She was sitting with a friend who also happened to be a friend of mine. So I thought, well, why not? Went up to their table. Introduced myself. Tried not to make a fool of myself." A faraway look filled his eyes. "Then we started talking about music and I was okay. We talked about all kinds of things that night. Loneliness. God. Forgiveness."

Paul offered Dodie a shy grin. "You know me and the Lord talk often about forgiveness. Anyway, when I got home, I wrote her a letter and she wrote me back. We kept it up for a while. Then I went down to visit her this winter and we hit it off." His face lit up. "And the rest is history."

"Well, I'd love to see her." Dodie felt a flutter in her heart at the thought of meeting a woman whose music had always touched her. Helen's soulful lyrics and heartfelt singing seemed to give voice to the very things she herself couldn't express. "What time should I come?"

"Seven. Eight. Up to you. Just make sure you bring some eggs like you usually do. And maybe some of those cranberry-and-orange muffins. Helen will love those."

"Right." Dodie tried to imagine a woman who had probably dined in the finest restaurants enjoying her homemade muffins. She was about to say something else when a movement caught her eye. A man. Tall. Dark hair. Commanding presence. And he was winding his way past the honey seller, the quilt lady and the man selling antler carvings, heading toward her and Paul.

Her heart stuttered and she felt a tinge of dismay.

She had thought that Jace wouldn't come here. She had thought that here, at least, she was safe from seeing him.

Today Jace wore blue jeans, a faded chambray shirt and a canvas coat. He blended in very well.

And he looked less like a corporate lawyer and more like the man she had once cared for. The man she no longer belonged to.

A residual pain pierced her heart. She had to get out of here.

But just as she was about to make a sharp left turn

toward Honey Bee Mine, Jace was in front of her, and it would look rude to walk around him.

And just at that moment Paul noticed him, as well.

"Well, hello, Jace," Paul said. "I heard you were back in town."

"And I heard congratulations are in order," Jace said, flashing Paul a dazzling smile.

Paul's grin ran from ear to ear. "Yeah. Thanks. I think I found a woman who doesn't mind listening to me foolin' on my guitar all hours of the night. God is good. All the time." He strummed his guitar as if to underline each statement.

"And I heard she's a singer," Jace continued.

Dodie frowned. How did he know so quickly? She had just found out herself.

"That she is. Better'n me." Paul looked him over. "So…Jace Scholte. Working for Carson MacGregor. Your dad would be proud."

Jace simply nodded, as if he wasn't quite sure what to make of Paul's statement.

"I would meet your dad, once in a while, when he'd go to the local coffee shop." Paul smiled. "He always had his Bible with him. Always read it, hoping someone would ask him more about it. He was a good man, your dad."

"Well, thanks for that," Jace said.

"I heard you got sent back here to clean up the mess Harvey left at the law office?"

"Hopefully. I'd like to restore Riverbend's faith in Carson and his firm."

Paul nodded. "Well, Carson's a good man. That boy of his is a pistol, though."

Jace chuckled. "I work with him now."

"Really? Chuck MacGregor? A lawyer like his daddy?"

Paul shook his head. "The Lord's mysterious ways never cease to confound me." He turned to Dodie. "So, you still coming tonight?"

"Of course. I wouldn't miss it," Dodie said with a forced smile, rubbing her arms against a sudden chill.

Paul turned to Jace. "You want to come, too?"

Dodie angled her body away from Jace and shot a frown at the singer, giving him an imperceptible shake of her head. She didn't want Jace along. Bad enough that he showed up here, where she thought she was safe from him, now he had to be intertwined into her social life?

It was too hard.

"My wife just moved here," Paul was saying. "I was telling Dodie she gets kind of lonely. Would be nice if we could have a couple over for company."

Dodie kept her gaze fixed firmly on Paul, hoping Jace would be put off by his torn blue jeans, his stained jacket worn and frayed at the cuffs, and his scuffed boots.

"Yeah. Why not?" Jace replied.

Dodie's heart plunged. She would have backed out immediately but for the fact that she would hurt Paul's feelings. Plus, she desperately wanted to meet one of her favorite singers.

"That's just great," Paul said. Then, with a smile and a wave, he strolled off, strumming another song, blissfully unaware of the chaos he'd just created.

She turned to Jace, ready to talk him out of coming. "You may as well know, Paul's place is…rustic at best. He lives way out east. Right along the river. You don't have to feel obligated to come."

"Obligated? Are you kidding? Miss a chance to meet Helen Lennox? I don't think so."

Dodie sighed. She knew her actions could be seen as

selfish. But in truth, it was self-preservation. She needed to create a time and space that Jace wasn't a part of if she was going to carry on working on the fundraiser.

Each time she saw him it grew harder and harder to maintain a casual attitude toward him. To act as if nothing had happened between them. As if he didn't matter to her....

"Besides," Jace continued, "I've been tapped to talk to him about singing at the fundraiser. The organizers thought it would be neat if he did what he does here. Walking around, singing old folk tunes and gospel music. So this works out perfectly." His glance skated over her, and for a moment she wondered if he felt as uncomfortable around her as she did around him.

"Do you know the way to Paul's place?" Jace asked.

Dodie made a point of looking at her watch. "Wow, look at the time. I've got a bunch of people to talk to yet." She lifted her gaze. "I'll see you later, I guess."

"I don't know how to get to Paul's place. Can I ride with you?"

Spending half an hour in the intimacy of a car? No way.

"Why don't you follow me?"

Jace frowned. "That doesn't make sense."

"Then you can leave whenever you want. In case you get bored."

"I doubt I'll get bored. Besides, I thought your car was at the mechanics, that's why you walked to my place for the meeting this week."

Dodie thought how her car had sputtered on the way here. She had to bring it back to the mechanic again. Obviously something was still wrong.

"Okay, then," she said, conceding defeat. "Meet me at my place at seven-thirty and we'll take your fancy BMW."

Two women hurried past them, jostling Jace. His shoulder brushed hers, and it was as if a live spark jumped between them.

Before he jerked away, however, Dodie caught the woodsy scent of his aftershave and her stomach knotted up with memory.

It was the same brand he always wore, the brand she had bought when they started dating because she disliked the brand he used until then.

Wannabe rich-guy cologne, she'd called it. The same kind Chuck MacGregor always used.

She swallowed and edged away. "I…I should get going. I've got to talk to a few more people. About some more donations."

Jace glanced at the clipboard in her hands. "Looks like you've been busy."

"I know how important this is to you."

"Hey, I wanted to talk to you about that. I think I came out kind of harsh." He lowered his voice and touched her arm.

Without thinking, she jerked her arm back just as he was about to say more. His face grew hard and he took a step back. "Sorry. I wasn't thinking."

Dodie's neck grew warm. He seemed to think she was upset with him because he had crossed an invisible boundary. He had. But he didn't need to know that her reaction was because of another unbidden emotion—attraction.

She tamped the feeling down and opted for a slightly injured air, building on his response. "That's okay. I have a wide personal space."

Jace's light frown reminded her that this wasn't always so. When they dated they'd held hands, walked with their arms linked, and sat in church with his arm over her shoulder, her hand cradled in his.

Don't go there. Don't go there.

"I'll see you tonight." She spun around and strode away as fast as she could, trying to outrun her memories and her emotions.

Chapter Four

Jace raised his fist to knock on Dodie's apartment door.

What was he doing? Did he have some kind of masochistic streak?

She wasn't interested in him anymore. She had made that abundantly clear.

Nor was she going to tell him what had happened all those years ago.

He should go.

And then what? Act as if everything between them was fine, over and done with, even though they had never even come close to discussing why she left?

He rapped on the door and stood back, wishing he didn't feel so nervous. He had done nothing wrong. Lest he forget, he was the one who'd been left behind. He resolved to relax and try to enjoy the evening.

He heard the sound of a deadbolt opening, then another lock. Dodie finally opened the door a crack and looked at him from behind a chain. She had a towel wrapped around her head and, from what he could see, was wearing a sweat suit. "Oh…you" was all she said.

He wasn't early. In another life, Dodie would have been scolding him for being late. But that was Dodie before. He felt he was constantly reminding himself that the meticulous Dodie he'd once dated was long gone.

The door opened again and Dodie stepped back from the door, toweling her hair. "I'll be a while longer." Her voice held the faintest note of challenge as she closed the door, but Jace chose not to acknowledge it. He simply nodded as he glanced around her apartment.

A beanbag chair slouched in one corner, and a worn Victorian couch with scrolled woodwork sat beside it. The lamps were covered with gauzy scarves, and though it was early spring, Christmas lights sparkled along the ceiling.

The thrift store decor was a far cry from her tidy dorm room in college. As was the homey scent of muffins hanging in the apartment. The old Dodie never baked.

She continued towel-drying her hair, angling her chin toward the living room. "Make yourself at home. There's not much to read. Some magazines on the coffee table but I doubt they'd be your style." She then disappeared into the other room.

While he heard the whirring of a blow-dryer in the background, Jace ambled into the tiny living room.

A few celebrity magazines were scattered on the coffee table. He picked one up, drawn by the hint of scandal promised by the headlines. The rest of the magazines slithered aside and he caught a glimpse of what looked like a psychiatry textbook.

Curious, he picked it up and leafed through it. Notes in Dodie's peculiar handwriting dotted the margins. Passages were highlighted in pink, yellow and blue. As he turned the next page, a piece of paper, also covered with Dodie's scribbles, fell out.

More notes.

He put the paper back where it belonged, closed the book and covered it again with the magazines.

Was Dodie going back to school? And where? There was no college within one hundred miles of Riverbend.

Or could she be taking a correspondence course?

He wished he felt confident enough to ask her what she was taking. At the same time, he felt the tiniest glimmer of hope. Maybe the honor student, the recipient of numerous scholarships, hadn't been completely subsumed by the new Dodie.

In the far corner of the living room sat a rickety desk holding a laptop decorated with colorful decals. The desk overflowed with papers, magazines and some more textbooks. Above the laptop, close to the phone, hung a large wall calendar. The days were scribbled with dozens of notes in different colored pens, showing her work schedule and, it seemed, a variety of other notes about groceries, appointments and reminders.

In spite of his curiosity, he pulled his attention away from the calendar, feeling as if he was intruding on a very personal part of her life.

The sun was just going down and the town lights were flickering on as he glanced out the large window of her living room. He knew, once they were out of the town limits, he would be able to see the stars.

A memory tugged at his consciousness. He and Dodie lying on the still-warm hood of her car, tracing out constellations in the sky. Dodie had tried to educate him about Cassiopeia, the Big and Little Dippers, tried to get him to find the stars Deneb and Vega.

But he was far more interested in trying to steal a kiss than gaze at stars.

Jace spun away from the window. In one way he wished he could forget her as easily as Dodie seemed to have forgotten him. The last time he was in Riverbend, he hardly saw her. He had thought he was over her. But when he returned to the city he couldn't seem to get her out of his mind.

So when Carson asked him to take on this job, a part of him thought it would be a chance to either confront Dodie or put the past behind him completely.

"Okay. We can go." Dodie came around the corner, and when Jace saw her he felt an unwelcome jolt of pleasure. Instead of her usual mix-and-unmatch clothes, she had opted for a simple off-white shirt, a brown corduroy blazer and blue jeans. A gauzy orange scarf added a splash of color.

She looked like the Dodie he knew. The Dodie he had once cared so deeply for.

"Oh wait. I forgot." She ducked into the miniscule kitchen off the living room and returned with a rectangular plastic container. "I promised Paul muffins and I better deliver."

"I still can't picture you baking," he said lightly.

"Let's just say I've picked up some good habits," Dodie said. "Shall we go?"

They walked in silence to the car. As Jace held the door open for Dodie, she gave him a wry smile. "Still a gentleman," she said.

"My mama taught me well," he answered, still holding the door as she slipped in with a graceful motion. He gently closed the door behind her, as if afraid to disturb the very tentative nature of the moment.

Jace had found an old CD of Helen Lennox, and as they drove out of town and into the darkness of the country, her deep, soulful voice filled the silence lying between Dodie and Jace.

And in that silence he felt a tiny spark of anticipation.

He leaned forward to look up at the sky. Stars winked back at him and he released his breath on a sigh.

"I missed this," he murmured, taking another quick glance upwards. "You can't see the stars in the city."

Dodie leaned forward herself. "We should be able to see Deneb by now. Orion is gone for the summer."

"I couldn't find it the first time you tried to point it out to me—I doubt I could find it now."

She gave him a curious glance. The green glow of the dashboard lights lent an eerie quality to her features. But the way her hair hung loose around her face made her feel as if the intervening years had slipped away. Once again they were two country kids, taking a break from the city and their endless studies to look at the stars. Taking a moment to appreciate God's creation and to marvel at the depth and breadth of it. They had some of their best talks lying on a blanket side by side in some farmer's field, hands intertwined, looking up at a sky sprinkled with diamonds.

"Dodie." He spoke her name softly as he took a breath and a chance. "Do you remember when—"

"You have to really look out for Paul's driveway," Dodie interrupted, turning away from him. "If you don't know where it is it will sneak up on you. The first time I drove up here, I got so lost. I backtracked a bunch of times, but eventually I found it. Paul never let me forget it. I'm sure he'll tease me again. He likes to do that. Throw the past in my face." An awkward silence filled the car when Dodie finally stopped babbling. She kept her face straight ahead and clasped her hands tightly on her lap.

"Are you okay?" he asked. Why had she been going on about directions and Paul?

"Yeah. I'm fine. Just want to make sure you don't get lost."

Paul's place was a good fifteen minutes away yet, but as Jace caught another glimpse of her tightly pressed lips and rigid jaw, he guessed something else was going on.

Frustration grabbed him with a tight fist. Every overture he made toward her she blatantly ignored.

It was as if she seemed eager to remind him at every turn that the past was behind them.

He shouldn't have asked to come along on this drive. If he was honest, seeing Helen was simply an excuse to spend time with Dodie in a casual situation.

He was obviously wasting his time.

"Turn up ahead," Dodie said, pointing.

Jace peered into the area lit up by his lights, but all he could see was tall, dry grass.

"Slow down. You'll see it."

Jace did as he was told, and as he looked he saw a dirt trail leading off the road.

"Are you sure?"

"I told you it was hard to find."

Jace turned onto the trail, and soon they were swallowed up by the trees looming above them. The lights of his vehicle wavered as he bounced over the track.

A few minutes later, the trees fell away, and ahead of them Jace could see rectangles of golden light shimmering from a log building in a small clearing directly ahead. A pair of dogs bounded down the driveway, darting in and out of the lights of his vehicle.

"Don't worry about the dogs," Dodie said, as Jace hit the brakes. "They're pretty vehicle-savvy."

Jace pulled up beside a fairly new pickup truck and cut the engine. "So, I'm guessing this is the right place."

"Of course," Dodie said, slipping her purse over her shoulder. "I wouldn't steer you wrong."

He let the comment slide as he got out himself and followed her up the walk. A light flicked on outside and the large wooden door of the log house opened. Paul stood in the doorway, the light inside the house casting him in silhouette. The dogs jumped around him but stayed away from Dodie and Jace.

"Come in, come in." Paul beckoned. "Just ignore the dogs. They'll settle down once they realize you're not going to feed them." He gave them a huge smile and took Jace's jacket as they stepped inside. "So, welcome to my home."

Jace's first impression was of light and warmth as he followed Dodie and Paul down the narrow hall into the house. The scent of cinnamon vied with the smell of wood burning in the squat black stove directly ahead of them.

To the right he caught a glimpse of wooden kitchen cabinets and a large oak table with chairs pushed around it.

Ahead and to the left lay the large living room. A leather couch and love seat faced each other. From an overstuffed recliner a tall, lithe woman raised herself and glided over to join Paul. In spite of the plaid, oversize shirt, fitted blue jeans and bare feet, she exuded grace and dignity. Her blond hair, now tinged with gray, was loosely tied back from a face devoid of makeup. A simple pair of earrings glinted from her earlobes.

Diamonds, Jace guessed.

"Honey, this is Dodie, the girl I was telling you all about," Paul said, putting his hand on Dodie's shoulder. "And this is Jace."

"Welcome, both of you. Good to have you here."

Jace tried not to feel dumbstruck. The face smiling at him was one he'd seen only on album covers and on the television screen when she deigned to do the occasional special. The voice was one he'd listened to many times. To imagine that he'd ever meet her out here in Riverbend seemed surreal.

"Dodie, I know you drink hot chocolate," Paul said, as he took the container of muffins Dodie had brought along. "Jace, what will you have? Coffee? Tea?"

"Coffee sounds great. Black, please."

"You all go settle in the living room and I'll be right back. Helen, you want anything?"

"I'll have the same as Dodie," she said, then turned and led the way to the living room.

"Paul tells me you're collecting for the fundraiser," Helen said, as she sank into a large, overstuffed recliner with her trademark grace.

Dodie nodded, looking as starstruck as Jace felt. A crack in her flippant facade. "We both are," she said, sitting at one end of the leather couch. Jace chose the opposite end of the couch and tried to relax.

"So tell me about this fundraiser," Helen said. With her hands casually perched on the armrests she looked, for all the world, like some regal monarch on vacation. "What's the cause?"

Jace glanced at Dodie, then realized she was expecting him to speak.

"Riverbend hopes to establish a building dedicated to crisis counseling," he said, struggling to act normal. "Currently the town's crisis counseling service shares office space, which isn't conducive to the privacy of their clients. Plus, they would like to expand and hire a few more counselors."

"That sounds like they would need ongoing funding rather than a one-shot fundraiser," Helen mused.

"The center has the funding in place from the government in partnership with the town for the ongoing operations," Jace said, warming to the subject. "They just don't have the proper facility. Depending on how well the fundraiser does, we would also hope to set up a foundation for donations that would help maintain the day-to-day running of the Center." He exhaled slowly. "And we'd like to make the fundraiser an annual thing to supplement any funding the foundation would get from the government and private donations."

Helen nodded and granted Jace a warm smile. "Sounds like you're well informed." She turned to Dodie. "And what's your role in this venture?"

"I'm collecting donations for the auction." She shot Jace a challenging look. "Actually, Jace and I are having a little contest to see who gets the most."

"Who's winning?" Helen asked, with a touch of humor.

Dodie shrugged and looked away again. "We won't know until it's over."

"Here's our refreshments," Paul announced, entering the room bearing a tray. He passed them around and then sat down in his rocker. "So, what did I miss?"

"Jace was telling me about the fundraiser," Helen said, taking a delicate sip of her hot chocolate.

"So what did you need to talk to me about, Jace?" Paul asked. His chair creaked as he rocked back and forth.

"We wanted to see if you would be willing to sing at the fundraiser."

Paul nodded his head slowly, as if considering. "Why?"

Jace glanced at Dodie, wondering if she would participate, but she was blowing into her hot chocolate, her eyes lowered.

"You're known in the community, enjoyed and appreciated," Jace said, repeating what he'd been told. He cradled the ceramic coffee cup in his hands. "The organizers thought it would be a unique touch if you did what you do at the farmer's market. Walk around and serenade the people attending."

Paul nodded. "Do you have other entertainment?"

"Not really. We've got a speaker booked and the auction and you."

"Sounds a bit thin."

Jace shrugged. He had thought so, too, but the organizers were concerned the evening would go too long if they added anything else. "That's where you come in."

Paul waved his hands. "What you should do is get Helen here to sing."

Jace hardly dared let his eyes meet Helen's for fear she might think that was exactly what he was up to. "Well… she's retired…and we don't want to intrude…" He scrambled to find a polite way to acknowledge the request yet let Helen know they didn't want to take advantage of her. He blamed his lapse on still trying to absorb the fact that he was sitting close to the actual Helen Lennox herself. He pulled himself together and tried again. "My purpose this evening is to speak with you."

Paul frowned. "Helen hasn't retired. She's just taking a break. And she's a great singer. She's released dozens of albums."

Helen leaned over and rested one slender hand on Paul's arm, interrupting his defense of her. "I think what Mr. Scholte is trying to say is he doesn't want to impose on his relationship with you."

She turned back to Jace. "This crisis center. Exactly what kind of counseling do they do?"

Jace thought back to the material he had been given and studied. He was about to explain when Dodie spoke up.

"Spousal abuse. Rape victims. Victims of other crimes," she answered. "The kinds of situations requiring intervention and cooperation with police yet also maintaining privacy, discretion and often protection for the victim."

Jace stared at her. He didn't think she knew anything about the center. And then his mind ticked back to the books he found on her table and her desk. A tiny glimpse into another part of her life.

She was an enigma.

Helen asked another question. Dodie answered. Paul interjected from time to time, but Jace sat back, watching Dodie, more than happy to let her speak for a change.

She was leaning back, her hands gripping the coffee mug, an unfamiliar glint in her eye, a surprising hardness to her features. Where had that come from? What did it mean?

The talk moved from the center to Riverbend. Helen asked Dodie about the town and the people.

"It's a great place to live," Dodie replied. "I moved away for a while, but the city didn't appeal to me. Too many people…too many bad memories."

Her words, spoken in an icy tone, were like a splash of cold water to Jace. He was a part of those memories.

He could only guess that the bad memories were connected to her sudden disappearance. But what could they be, and why had she never told him?

He tried to catch her eye, hoping he could get even a tiny glimpse into the past.

But she avoided his gaze.

He couldn't sit here anymore. Helen or no, he had to get out.

"Excuse me," he murmured as he got up.

He didn't know where his jacket was and didn't care. He stepped outside, shivering. Winter was gone, but chill remnants still lingered in the night air.

The dogs got up, tongues lolling, happy for the diversion. Jace gave them absent pats on their heads then shoved his hands in his pockets. He trudged down the driveway, the dogs' exuberance a stark counterpoint to his own funk.

He got as far as his car, away from the light of the house. He leaned against the hood and stared up into the inky blackness spangled with stars. He thought of Dodie's astronomy lessons and found the North Star. From there, he traced the Big Dipper, then found the Little Dipper. Just like Dodie had taught him.

Stop thinking about her, he told himself. She doesn't seem to want to think about you.

He reached back for other memories that didn't contain her essence, and the words of a Psalm drifted into his mind.

"When I consider the heavens," he murmured, "the moon and the stars which you have ordained…"

Jace let the last words come out on a sigh. He couldn't remember the rest.

Forgive me, Lord, he prayed, guilt sifting past the words he tried to dredge from his past. *Forgive me for not spending the time I should with You.*

But even as he prayed, he felt his attention being drawn, against his will, back to the woman in the house. The woman he couldn't forget. The woman who had just implied that her time with him held bad memories for her.

He slammed his hand against the hood of the car.

Why couldn't he let go? Why did he insist on hanging on? On trying to figure her out?

She hadn't let him in previously…she certainly wasn't about to let him in now.

He drew in a long, slow breath and kept his eyes on the stars. He just had to stick around Riverbend a little longer, he thought. Then he could go back to Edmonton. Back to his own law practice and business. Back to the long hours and the endless jockeying for position.

Well, that was the way it was. If he wanted to make something of himself and get ahead, that's what it would take.

Besides, he owed it to Carson, who had helped him out in so many ways. Carson was the one who had helped pay his tuition, and Carson was the one who was there when Dodie left, offering his support and encouragement.

"You okay out here?" Paul called out as he approached Jace.

"Yeah. I'm okay." Jace pushed himself away from the car and turned to face Paul, who was holding his coat.

"I thought you might want this."

"Thanks." Jace slipped the coat on and shivered a bit. "It's cooler out than I'd realized."

"Thought I would join you. Let the women have some time to gab." Paul leaned against Jace's car, his arms folded over his chest, looking as if settling in for a chat. "Peaceful out here, isn't it?"

"Yeah. I missed this—living in the city."

"I couldn't live there. Being here, away from people, away from noise and expectations, keeps me sane." He gave Jace a quick smile.

Jace didn't reply, sensing none was needed. For a moment they stood side by side, silence surrounding them save for the occasional howl of a coyote shivering into the night.

"Helen and Dodie seem to be hitting it off," Paul said, finally. "I'm glad. Helen could use some company."

"How does Helen like living out here?" Jace let loose one of the easier questions that had been spinning around his mind.

"She likes the quiet and the privacy." Paul sighed and looked up at the stars, as well. "She's had a tough go the past few years. Lots of pain. I think she's healing now."

His ambiguous reply only created more questions, but Jace wanted to respect Helen and Paul's privacy. He was only a figure passing through their lives. He had no right to intrude.

"She's a bit like Dodie," Paul continued, his voice thoughtful. "That's why I thought I would come out here. Let them talk a bit in private."

"How is she like Dodie?"

Paul turned to Jace. "You and Dodie used to date, didn't you?"

"Yeah. How did you know?"

"Well, this is Riverbend. Your secret is my secret and all that." Paul's eyes flashed in the darkness. "You're not the one who hurt her, are you?"

Was it his imagination, or did he catch the faintest hint of aggression in the soft-spoken man's voice?

Jace sighed. "I don't think so…but I don't know."

"What do you mean, you don't know?"

"One day we were dating, everything was fine. I had no idea anything was wrong. Then, the next day, I try to call her and she's gone."

"Gone?"

"Gone. Not at home. Not at school. A day later, I'm panicking, thinking something horrible happened. I'm about to round up a couple of friends to go looking for her, when her mom calls me. She tells me Dodie's in London." Jace lifted his hands in a gesture of frustration as his words spilled out of a place long kept repressed. "I didn't even know she knew anyone in London. And what was she doing there anyway?"

"Did you try to go after her?"

"I would have, except I didn't have a lot of money, so I tried to call her. Write her. Sent messages via her sister, Janie and her parents. But she didn't answer my calls, she didn't write. Nothing." He pressed his lips against the unexpected anger. He pulled in a steadying breath, reaching for calm. "So, yeah. I tried."

"How long did she stay away?"

"A year and a month. Then she came back here to Riverbend. But didn't contact me at all."

"She still means something to you, doesn't she?"

Jace stared sightlessly into the night, testing his feelings. "It's been too long without anything being said, without any explanations. Whatever we may have had is over." He was lying, but he hoped that if he said it enough times, thought it enough times, it would be true.

Paul nodded, as if he understood. Jace slanted him a sidelong look, surprised at what he had just told a virtual stranger. But he seemed to be no stranger to Dodie, and maybe Jace had harbored some faint hope that Paul could enlighten him.

"Relationships are a source of frustration, but they can be one of great security, as well," Paul said.

"How did you and Helen—" Jace let the question drop. "Sorry. That's none of my business."

"How did we get together?" Paul laughed. "Don't worry, I thought the same. I've known and admired the great Helen Lennox for years, and when I met her I was as tongue-tied as anyone else. And then when we got to talking about music, I was a bit more comfortable." His tone softened. "But when I looked deep into her eyes and saw the hurt there, she became simply a lonely woman in pain. And I knew I could help her."

"How?"

"I asked the right questions. And I listened. I had to work awful hard on Helen to get her to trust me," he said quietly. "I didn't think I'd be able to help her since she was hurt so badly. But thankfully, with God's help, Helen found peace and value in herself again."

Jace wondered what had hurt Helen, but in spite of Paul's forthright answers, he knew better than to pry.

"I hope Dodie and Helen can help each other," Paul continued.

He threw out his ambiguous comment so casually, Jace almost missed the undercurrent of concern in Paul's voice.

"What do you mean?"

Paul rested the palms of his hands on the car behind him, focusing on the stars above. "Dodie has the same look Helen does."

"What look is that?"

Paul drummed his fingers on the hood of the car, then pushed himself away. "Like her trust has been broken."

His words sent a chill through Jace's body. He felt as if he should know exactly what Paul was talking about.

He was about to ask Paul more when the dogs started howling and Paul's attention was diverted to them. "Hush, you two. It's just coyotes." He pushed himself away from the car. "We better get them inside before they get all wound up. Once they do they don't quit."

Paul whistled for the dogs and headed toward the house.

Jace followed him inside, letting the warmth chase away the chill of the night, questions lingering.

Dodie and Helen were still talking, their murmuring

conversation creating a welcoming sound. Jace heard Dodie laugh, the sound generating an answering twinge of melancholy. Dodie used to laugh all the time.

He and Paul stepped into the living room just as Dodie got up from the couch, smiling at Helen. She hadn't seen him yet.

Her face was animated, her eyes bright and as she talked, her hand sketched vague pictures in the air. "So I'll have to talk to the organizers and see what we can arrange."

Dodie caught sight of Paul first, and her smile deepened.

But he could tell the moment her eyes fixed on his. Had he imagined that flicker of haunting pain in her blue eyes?

Were Paul's words making him see something that hadn't been there before?

At any rate, as soon as their eyes met, it was as if someone flipped a switch and her eyes grew distant.

And Jace felt his frustration return.

She turned to Helen and held out her hand. "Thanks so much for your hospitality. I so appreciate the visit."

Guess we're going, Jace thought.

Jace glanced at Paul, wondering if he should ask once again about him singing at the fundraiser. But he didn't want to seem like he was nagging, so he let it go.

Now that he had met Paul face-to-face, he could deal with that issue with one phone call.

"Thank you, as well," he said, also shaking Helen's and then Paul's hand. "I enjoyed myself."

"You two come again," Paul said, shooting Jace a faint wink. "You're welcome any time."

"Yes, please, come again," Helen added, giving Dodie an extrawarm smile.

Dodie returned the smile, took her coat from Paul, then, with one final goodbye, left the house. She slipped her coat on, then walked ahead of Jace, her arms crossed over her midsection, her head down.

They drove in silence for a few minutes when Jace thought he heard a muffled sniff coming from across the car. Then, as he glanced surreptitiously over, he saw Dodie's hand sneak up to wipe moisture from her cheeks.

She was crying.

He swallowed, unsure of what to do. He was never good with a woman's tears, let alone the sadness of a girl who was once so important to him.

He kept silent, however, fairly sure she wouldn't want his attention, but when she dabbed at her cheeks again, he couldn't stand it any longer.

"Dodie, what's wrong?"

She became stock-still, as if his question was an unwelcome intrusion. But she said nothing.

"Are you okay?"

She drew in a shuddering breath and looked ahead, a small concession.

"No. I'm not." Her admission was an anguished whisper, as if the words were dragged from her.

Jace's heart flipped slowly over. Finally, he thought. She's finally ready to open up to me. He was about to press her for more information when she spoke again.

"But I don't want to talk about it, okay?" she said, drawing in a ragged breath.

Jace glanced at her, but she kept her gaze directed straight ahead, her posture stiff and unyielding.

He couldn't let this sit. Couldn't leave it at this. "Why not?"

She sliced the air between them with her hand, cutting off further conversation. "No, Jace. No more questions."

"But, Dodie—"

"I can't. Not now. Please." Her voice broke on that last word and Jace's heart ached with yearning. He wanted to stop the car, reach over and pull her close.

Instead he kept driving, clinging to the tentative nature of her last comment. In spite of her reluctance, he felt as if he had witnessed a breakthrough. A glimpse into whatever it was that Dodie was hiding.

He clung to that all the way back to Riverbend. He wasn't going to let things go now. Not after this.

Chapter Five

"**I**'ve got this great travel mug I can donate." Chester at the Farm and Feed Supply held up a plastic bag with a silver mug inside. "It's got the name of the business on it," he said, setting it down on the counter in front of Jace. "Will I get more advertising out of the deal?"

Jace eyed the cheap metal mug and mentally sighed. Chester's mug was hardly going to put him in the running to meet Dodie's challenge.

"Everyone who donates will have their name put on a card on the wall in the arena and on the event program." Jace pulled out his PDA. "Would you like to buy tickets, as well?"

"I heard that if you donate something, tickets are free."

"Not true," Jace said decisively, glancing at the mug that couldn't have cost Chester more than three dollars, which might, if people were feeling generous, bring in five dollars.

"So how much are tickets," Chester asked.

"Seventy-five dollars apiece."

Chester whistled as he leaned his elbows on the counter. "You're not going to get many people coming at that price."

"It's a fundraiser," Jace explained patiently.

"I pay that much to go to a concert. Don't think it's much worth my while to pay that much to eat half-baked food."

"We've got a great caterer," Jace replied. "The food will be amazing."

"Yeah, well. I'll see."

"Don't wait too long," Jace said, picking the mug up off the counter. "Tickets are getting hard to come by." Which was patently untrue. Ticket sales were sluggish at best, but Jace held out hope the big rush would come the last couple of weeks.

"We'll see," Chester said, drumming his fingers on the scarred wooden counter.

"Hey, Jace. Don't tell me you've taken up farming as well as lawyering?"

Jace felt a large hand drop on his shoulder and he turned to face a heavyset man whose worn plaid shirt strained at the mismatched buttons. The stained cowboy hat on his head was dented and frayed, but his blue jeans were so new they were still stiff.

"Aiden Ochremchuk. Good to see you again. How are the kids?" Jace shook Aiden's other hand, or rather had his hand shook. His old friend did nothing by halves.

Aiden released Jace's fingers but kept his other hand on Jace's shoulder. "Driving me nuts. That's why I had to get out."

Jace still had to smile. Though he'd kept up with his high school friend, he still struggled to reconcile the resident class clown of his high school years with a settled father of three children. He was a lot further ahead of the game than Jace was.

The thought gave him a momentary pang. Had things

gone the way he had planned, he and Dodie could have had at least one child by now.

"And I heard you're doing some serious canvassing for this big shindig comin' up?"

"Yes." Jace nodded, pushing the memories away. "Would you have anything to donate?"

"Already talked to your partner in crime. Dodie finagled a trip for four down the river in Dad's jet boat. I'm driving."

Jace had to smile. "Is that safe?"

Aiden waved away his concerns. "I'm a responsible father of three kids with another one on the way. There's no way I want to jeopardize their future. Besides, Sally would kill me if something happened to me." Aiden laughed. "But that Dodie, she's got the makings of a good lawyer. She even got Dad to throw in a filet of beef barbecue at the Riverbend campground on top of it. And Sally is making dessert." He laughed again, shaking his head.

Jace gave Aiden a weak smile. "Then I guess you're tapped out. Thanks so much for your generosity." This boat trip was exactly what he'd been angling for. Unique, interesting and something the ordinary person couldn't purchase anywhere else.

"Don't worry," Aiden said, pulling out a wallet from his back pocket. "Dodie let slip about your little game." Aiden pulled out a wrinkled piece of paper and handed it to Jace. "Get your secretary to type this up."

Jace glanced down at the scribbled writing on the paper. It said that the Ochremchuk Family Ranch was good for one weekend for two at the ranch, complete with home-cooked meals and horseback riding.

"This is fantastic, Aiden," he said with a huge grin.

"Got to keep things even. Can't have Dodie thinking

she's got one over on my good friend. Besides, I wouldn't mind seeing the two of you together again." Aiden adjusted his battered hat as he shook his head. "Always thought you would get married by now." He shot him a meaningful look as if hoping Jace would expand on his remark.

Jace's mind ticked back to the evening spent with Paul and Helen. On Sunday he had gone to church, but Dodie hadn't. He had hoped, by some small miracle, to try to talk to her. To build on the minuscule crumb she had given him.

But she hadn't come.

"Do you know how long you're sticking around town?"

Jace shook his head with a touch of regret. He liked working with Aiden and his father. They were interesting and both had a good sense of humor. Plus Bill and Aiden were always working on one deal or another, which kept the Riverbend branch of Carson's law firm busy. "As soon as I'm done, though, I'm back to the Edmonton office."

"I hope they get a decent replacement for you and not one like the guy before you. When I saw all those mistakes he made on that real-estate deal we put together eight months ago I wondered if the guy got his degree from a cereal box. I still can't believe Carson hired the guy. Sometimes I think Carson's too soft." Aiden tightened his hand on his shoulder. "And then I get his bill for work he does for me and I think, nope. Hard as nails." He laughed again, letting Jace know his comment was all in fun.

Jace saw the minute hand sweeping across the clock behind Chester and gave Aiden a quick smile, holding up the piece of paper. "Thanks a ton for this. I'll get my secretary, Callie, to make up a nice certificate for this."

Aiden's expression grew serious. "Think of it as a little

bribe so you'll consider staying here. Riverbend is a good place to raise a family. Your mom and dad thought so."

Jace might have been inclined to agree with him. If he was even remotely headed toward matrimony. After Dodie left, he hadn't found anyone he wanted to date more than a couple of times, let alone settle down with.

"Thanks, Aiden. I'll…I'll keep it in mind."

"You do that. And while I'm yammering away—" his jovial expression grew suddenly serious "—how's your mom?"

"She misses Riverbend but is glad to be back in Ontario with her family. Thanks for asking."

Aiden shook his head. "Your father was a good man. My dad always said he was a reminder to all of us about being content and treating people fair."

Jace felt a nudge of melancholy at Aiden's surprisingly serious words. His memories of his father were a mixed bag of the usual parent/child frustration over restrictions. All he remembered were the fights over money at home. Because his father didn't work, Jace never stopped to think about how he was received outside of the home.

But coming back here to Riverbend, especially since he'd been canvassing around the town, he'd been privy to other points of view about his father. Heard other stories of things his father did that his mother never gave him credit for.

And each little bit of information he gleaned gave him a new appreciation for his father. In spite of his disabilities, Rick Scholte had been involved in various aspects of the community and was respected and appreciated for his simple faith.

Jace tucked Aiden's paper in his pocket. "Thanks again. I should get going. Got to go to a meeting."

"You do that. I think you got a good chance to even up the score with Dodie," Aiden said. "And make sure you come by when you've got some time. Sally said she'd love to try a new recipe out on you."

"Sounds…intriguing."

"Good word," Aiden said with a knowing wink. "Take care."

Half an hour later Jace sauntered up the walk to Sheila Kippers's place, feeling pretty confident about his chances to best Dodie.

He rang the doorbell and she answered the door right away. Sheila had her hair down, and she wore a snug knit dress, full makeup and a smile that seemed to be more welcoming than it should—considering the divorcée was about seven years older than him.

"Come in, Jace. So good to see you." Her smile widened and she touched him lightly on the shoulder. "Dodie's already here." This was delivered with a faint note of regret that, it seemed, she expected him to share.

"Terrific," Jace said with false enthusiasm. He stepped into the house, giving Sheila a wide berth. "I need to talk to her, too."

Sheila's glistening lips formed a pout. "She's in the den. Just go down the stairs. Door's to your right. I'll be right back after I get us something to snack on."

"Do you have to check on your kids?" Jace asked, putting extra emphasis on the last word.

"They're staying overnight at a friend's place tonight. Sleepover."

"Lucky them." Jace made a quick getaway down the stairs. He suddenly felt just a little more uncomfortable around Sheila.

Dodie sat on the floor of a large, open room, papers spread around her, a pencil stuck between her teeth. Her fingers danced over the calculator buttons as her eyes gleamed. Today she wore her hair down, and her baggy pants and loose T-shirt were a welcome contrast to the overt display he'd just been subjected to.

"Hello there." He smiled warmly as he dropped into a recliner beside her.

Dodie's head spun around. "You might want to wipe that smile off your face. You're going down, Jace Scholte."

Her jaunty tone and suddenly cheerful demeanor gave Jace a thrill. She was acting like the old Dodie.

Jace dropped his own folder onto the low table in front of Dodie. "And what makes you so confident? You don't even know what donation I managed to get." He held her gaze and, to his surprise, she didn't look away.

"I highly doubt you can beat this." Dodie pulled out a piece of paper and laid it on the table in front of him. Jace saw Bill's and Aiden's names, and smiled.

In turn, he went to his own folder and pulled out a couple of papers he'd managed to type up and print before he left. "I'll see your boat trip from the Ochremchuks with this," he said, placing a gift certificate for a plasma television on top of the paper. Then he pulled out the paper he had just printed and dropped it on the stack. "And I'll raise you a weekend at the Ochremchuk ranch."

Dodie looked at the papers but to Jace's disappointment, she didn't seem fazed.

She twisted around and picked up several more papers. "Homemade quilt from the Quilter's Guild." She slapped one paper after another down on top of Jace's boat trip printout. "Handmade silver jewelry from Marcie at the farmer's market. Spa treatment at Arlene's. Custom-made stained-glass window. Collector doll and hand-sewn ward-robe." She looked smug as she continued down the list. "Hand-crafted dollhouse. Hand-painted stemware…"

Then she gave him a quick grin. "And I'm saving the best for when Sheila comes back."

Jace would have felt disappointed but for Dodie's bright eyes, her quick smile and the dimple winking at him from one cheek.

"Sounds like you've been busy. I'm impressed," he said, reaching over and picking up the top piece of paper. "You've put a lot of time and energy into this."

"I told you I was going to win," she said triumphantly.

Jace put the paper down and his eyes wandered to hers. To his surprise she didn't look away.

A lock of hair slipped over her cheek and without stopping to think, Jace reached over and brushed it away. Like he used to.

Then she caught his wrist, curling her fingers around it. Like she used to.

For a split second they were connected.

Jace's mind slipped back to that moment of weakness he saw in her during the car ride home. Questions swirled in his mind as he struggled with old, residual feelings.

"Dodie, I wish—"

"Here we are." Sheila bustled into the room with a tray of clinking glasses. "Refreshments for the evening."

Dodie dropped his hand as if it burned her, and her gaze retreated downward as she scurried back to the couch.

Jace felt like cursing Sheila's sudden arrival. Once again it seemed as if he had hovered on the threshold of discovery. As if one more moment would have slipped open the door into Dodie's secrets.

Sheila handed him a glass of soda. "Help yourself to

cookies or muffins," she said, pointing to the plate heaped with baked goodies. She stood in front of him for an extra moment, as if waiting for some kind of acknowledgment.

"Thanks." Jace glanced up at her and took a quick sip of soda, his eyes returning to Dodie.

But she was ignoring him, gathering up papers, shuffling them into piles.

Sheila pulled a chair closer to the low table and dropped her folder on it with a *thunk*.

"So, how did you do with your list, Sheila?" Jace asked.

Sheila looked from Dodie to Jace as if she sensed something happening between them.

"I got something from most everyone," she said, tapping a shining fingernail on her folder. "Gift certificates. And quite a few donations. Some clothes, some custom embroidery for a sweatshirt, tickets to the symphony in September and tickets to an Oilers hockey game in October. Box seats," she added with a satisfied grin.

"Wow. That's pretty good." Jace was impressed. Between what Dodie had collected, what he had managed to pull together, and Sheila's contributions, both the live and silent auctions looked to be a huge success.

"Is Paul singing during the dinner, as you hoped?" Sheila asked.

"I'm not sure…" Jace looked over at Dodie. "He was going to get back to you, wasn't he?"

Dodie nodded. "He called yesterday to tell me he wasn't going to sing."

Jace frowned. Why was Dodie looking as if she had just scored some major coup?"

"Helen Lennox is going to sing instead."

Jace and Sheila spoke up at once.

"Are you kidding?"

"Really?"

"How did you…what…" Jace sputtered, his mind ticking back to that evening. Helen hadn't given the slightest indication that she was interested in singing ever again, let alone for their fundraiser.

"That's unbelievable," Sheila said, with a trace of envy in her voice. "I didn't realize you knew her."

"I didn't. I met her when Jace and I went to visit her and Paul.

"I heard they got married. I thought it was just a rumor," Sheila huffed, twisting a strand of dark hair around her finger. "I can't imagine she would choose to live way out in the boonies in that cabin of his." She rolled her eyes at Jace as if he would understand.

"It's very cozy," Dodie said with a wistful tone. "And quiet. I think I could live there. Far away from people…"

Jace wondered at the note of yearning in her voice.

"So did Helen say what she was going to sing? Is she going to get her band to perform with her? Or is she flying solo?" Sheila grabbed a notebook and clicked her pen, glancing from Jace to Dodie, looking for more information.

"We didn't iron out all the details," Dodie replied, her smile lingering at the edge of her lips as she hugged her knees. "But I do believe she said something about Paul accompanying her."

"So it would be an acoustic set." Sheila clicked her pen again, then scribbled some notes. "Our ticket sales are going to go through the roof once word gets out. Between our speaker and Helen Lennox, this will be a sold-out event."

"I imagine." Dodie rested her chin on her knees then turned her head to look at Jace. "You do realize that this little coup, on top of all the other donations I've already gotten, puts me squarely in the lead."

"Do you want me to concede already?"

"How many more businesses are left on your list?" Dodie asked, a faintly taunting note filling her voice.

"A few."

"Probably the ones that didn't return your calls the first time? The ones that maybe have something, you know, like a T-shirt or a mug?"

Jace lifted his hands in a gesture of defeat. "Okay. I give up. You won."

"Won? Won what?" Sheila frowned at both of them, obviously puzzled.

"Dodie and I had a little contest going to see who would get the most valuable donations," Jace explained, setting his cup down on the table. "And I think she's won."

"Really? How interesting." Sheila's tone intimated she thought anything but. "Why wasn't I informed of this?"

"It was just between Jace and me," Dodie said. "I think he was scared I was going to quit on him, and he figured I needed the incentive."

"Little did I know," Jace said. "Especially now that you've managed to get Helen to come and sing. Congratulations. I'm very proud of you."

Dodie shrugged, but Jace saw a flush creep up her neck. The small hint of her discomfort gave him his second sliver of hope. And even better, he'd lost his challenge with her, which meant he got to take her out for dinner.

The three of them spent the rest of the evening sorting out the donations, deciding which ones needed certificates, and where to store the ones already received. As they catalogued the items, Jace grew more excited about the prospects of the fundraiser. It was going to be a roaring success and a huge feather in his cap.

Carson would be sure to take notice, he thought. Anything that put him in Carson's field of vision was a bonus.

"So where do we bring all the actual donations?" Dodie asked, getting to her feet.

"I'm going to suggest my office. I imagine that would probably be the most secure place to store them." Jace replied.

"Okay. I'll bring what I've got already."

Jace tried to catch her eye as she gathered up her papers, but she seemed to be ignoring him.

A pang of disappointment reverberated through him. Had he imagined that moment between them?

Chapter Six

Dodie glanced at the clock on her dashboard before she got out of the car. Jace's secretary told her that he wouldn't be back until twelve-thirty, which gave her twenty minutes.

The box holding the quilt was surprisingly heavy, and she'd had to park a ways down the street, so she was out of breath by the time she pushed her way through the large glass door into Jace's office.

"What have you got now?" Jace's secretary, Callie, asked, looking up as Dodie put the box onto the floor.

"The quilt." Dodie set the box down and caught her breath. "I didn't think that it would weigh so much."

Callie got up from her desk. "Do you need a hand?"

"I'll help her."

Dodie's heart shifted at the sound of Jace's deep voice. What was he doing here? He wasn't supposed to be back yet.

She felt a frisson of awareness when she caught his blue eyes looking down at her. Why was it that every time she saw him, the old feelings grew stronger?

And why was it that each moment they were together, she wavered between pleasure in his company and bittersweet regret?

"So this is the quilt?" he asked, bending down to pick up the box.

"If you don't mind putting it away, that'd be great." She took a step backward, toward the door. "I should get going anyway, so thanks."

"I'll bring it to the room, but you'll have to show me what to do with it."

Dodie was about to tell him she didn't care. But he had already headed down the hallway, and walking away would look rude, so she followed him.

He shouldered open the door behind which the rest of the auction items were stored. "As you can see, it's getting full in here, and I don't want it to get squashed, so do you have any ideas?" Jace asked.

"Most anyplace will do. Just make sure nothing gets stacked on top of it." Dodie glanced around the room. "Wow. Things are really picking up."

"Callie had most of the gift certificates typed up already, and we're still getting a few more donations in. We're going to have a full day just tagging everything, then another entire day setting it all up in the arena."

"I've got Steve to deliver his stained-glass window directly here. I have a bit of nagging to do to get some of the other stuff in, but I'm slowly getting my list done." Dodie couldn't help adding, "My very *extensive* list."

Jace set the box beside the boxed-up dollhouse Dodie had brought yesterday, then turned to her. "And speaking of your list, I owe you a dinner. I've been trying to get hold of you to arrange it, but you seem to be avoiding me." He arched an eyebrow at her. "Text messages? C'mon."

Dodie shrugged his comment aside. "Don't worry about dinner. It was a good incentive. You don't need to follow through."

"I honor my deals," Jace said. "So, how about this Saturday?"

Dodie let her eyes graze over him again, testing her reaction to him, and her stomach twisted as his eyes held hers. "I think I'm babysitting for Janie that night."

"You used that excuse the last time you weren't baby-sitting for Janie." Jace crossed his arms as if getting ready to challenge her.

"This time I am."

"I checked already. Janie, Luke and the kids are gone for the weekend. And your mother doesn't need you for anything." He quirked a brow. "And as far as I know, there's no special market day within a two-hour drive, nor are you working at Janie's coffee shop or the thrift store that night."

As she tried to hold his gaze, her mind slipped back to that evening in Sheila's basement. When he had touched her and she had thought her heart was going to jump out of her chest.

Then she had held his wrist, caught the scent of his cologne and something at the core of her being had shifted.

She had missed him so much it created an ache within her. An ache she couldn't act on.

So she had ignored his phone calls and messages about dinner. There was no way she could go out with him and pretend as if everything was fine.

"I'm not going to quit until you agree."

Why he was bothering with her?

His persistence created a spark of yearning, which she quickly quashed. If he knew…

"If you keep putting me off, I'm going to think something else is going on," he said. "And I'm a lawyer, I know how to ask questions…know how to find out secrets—"

"Okay. Fine." She glared at him, hating the pressure. But his comment about finding out secrets bothered her more. "I get to pick the place."

Jace raised his hands in a gesture of mock surrender. "How could I forget?"

She let her gaze rove over his suit and made a sudden decision.

"Why don't we do D.J.'s. Saturday night."

"D.J.'s? Not the Riverbend Inn?"

Dodie shook her head. "We'll do takeout and eat by the river."

"Okay. It's your choice. I'll pick you up at five o'clock."

Dodie thought that was the end of that. Until Jace took a step closer.

Don't step back, she thought. Don't move away. Stand your ground.

But she couldn't stop her breath from coming faster, her heart from pounding a little harder.

Jace frowned as if sensing her discomfort and touched her cheek. Just the faintest brush of his fingers, hearkening back to a time when it was his right to do so and she would have welcomed his touch.

"Are you afraid of me?"

She chanced another look into his eyes, then over his familiar features. In her mind she saw herself tracing the scar on the side of his face with her finger like she used to. Her way of letting him know that she saw the faint disfigurement as part of him.

If anything, the scar created an air of mystery and danger that Dodie knew still could smolder beneath Jace's now-benign expression.

"Did I do something to make you fearful of me?" he pressed.

She could see his heartbeat at the base of his neck, could smell the scent of his aftershave. She felt herself waver.

Then his cell phone rang and Dodie was spared.

He pulled it out of his pocket, frowned at it and then stepped away from her. "Sorry. I have to take this. It's Carson."

Dodie nodded, her pulse racing.

"I'll come for you on Saturday," he said. "Don't forget."

"I won't." And then she fled.

Blue jeans. T-shirt. Cardigan. Chunky necklace.

Dodie laid the clothes out on the bed and examined them once more. She and Jace were just going out for hamburgers, not a full-on date, yet she fretted about the color of the T-shirt, the cut of the blue jeans. Was the knee-length cardigan too much? Should she wear running shoes or the leather boots she found at the thrift store? Would Jace notice that the boots were secondhand? Would he care?

And why wasn't she wearing the orange silk shirt she had originally planned? Was she trying to prove something?

This was ridiculous.

She yanked on her blue jeans, slipped on the T-shirt, cardigan and necklace. She looked fine. A little more conservative than usual, but fine. Just fine.

In the bathroom, she applied a hint of mascara to her lashes, added a spritz of perfume and pulled her hair into a ponytail. Then she caught her reflection in the mirror. Her cheeks were flushed, her eyes bright.

She let her hair drop, her mind drifting back, once again, to that moment in Sheila's basement when Jace's hand had tangled in her hair.

How she had wished his hand would linger.

She yanked her hair back and twisted an elastic around it. Jace was living up to his obligations by taking her out. Nothing more was going on between them.

In a couple of months he would be gone. Back to his law firm in Edmonton and out of her life.

Her hands stilled and she felt a brush of sorrow.

Then she shook it off. He's not for you, Dodie Westerveld, she thought, as she marched into the living room to wait.

Ten minutes later she sat perched on the edge of her couch, paging mindlessly through a magazine she'd already read, trying not to look at the clock.

Jace was eight minutes late.

She tossed the magazine aside and walked to the window of her apartment, but there was no sign of his car.

Twenty minutes later, she had organized her spices and tidied her jewelry box. She looked around for something else to do, then shook her head.

No way was she going to wait around her apartment.

She grabbed her car keys from the hook hanging by the door, then yanked opened the door and stopped.

Jace stood directly in front of her, still wearing a suit, his face flushed and his hand lifted to knock.

"I'm so sorry," he said. He shoved his hand through his hair in a gesture that was so familiar it created a gentle ache in Dodie's heart. "I got a frantic call from Randy Webber, the chairman. Mr. Rialto, the fundraiser's speaker, might be canceling on us. Randy and I were trying to come up with a backup plan."

"No way." Dodie felt Jace's disappointment. Stuart Rialto had been as big a catch as Helen Lennox. He had been booked eighteen months in advance.

"It's not a definite, but we had to do some brainstorming. That's why I'm late."

"Have you come up with anything?"

"Randy is following through on a few possible replacements, though it's hard to find someone on such short notice."

"It would be such a disappointment if Rialto bailed."

"Yeah. But thanks to you we got Helen. And thanks to that, the ticket sales are going very well." He squirmed. "Sorry. I don't want to be talking about the fundraiser. And again, sorry I'm late. You look like you were just leaving?"

"I decided I didn't feel like waiting around." Dodie glanced at his suit. "I'm not going to hold you to this, though."

"You can. I've been looking forward to this."

"Hamburgers?"

"Haven't had a D.J.'s burger for years."

Dodie locked the door of her apartment behind her, then double-checked the door and the deadbolt.

"It's probably okay," Jace said with a trace of bemusement in his voice.

"Doesn't hurt to check." Dodie gave the door another rattle, then turned to Jace. "Shall we go?"

"I've got my car here. Unless you want to go in separate vehicles."

"No. You lost the contest. You can pay for gas." Dodie kept her tone carefree, but she couldn't repress an odd sense of excitement.

After they got their burgers, Dodie directed him to the park along the river.

While Dodie got out, Jace took a cardboard box and a blanket from the backseat of the car.

"Dessert," he said, holding up the box at her puzzled

look. "Strawberry cheesecake. Got it from the bakery during my lunch hour."

He remembered her favorite dessert.

Dodie felt a twinge of pleasure, and on the heels of that a flutter of anticipation.

Jace caught her gaze, and for a moment sparks arced between them.

She looked away.

"Can't wait." Dodie turned and walked over the spongy grass to a large aspen tree perched along the edge of the river. The sun warmed her shoulders through the material of her sweater. From the branches of one of the trees a robin sent his song into the spring air.

The idyllic setting eased Dodie's nerves.

"We can eat here," she said, pointing to a space under the tree.

Jace set the basket down, spread the blanket out and settled himself on one edge. Dodie eyed the blanket. "That's not very big."

"Big enough." Jace glanced at her and smiled. "You don't take up much space."

Dodie could have sat on the grass, but though the day had been unseasonably warm for spring, she knew the ground would still be damp.

So she gave in and sat down on the edge of the blanket, then opened the bag with her burger and fries. She bent over and took a deep sniff. "Burgers. So much more than just a fast food."

She was about to figure out what she was going to eat first—and how to eat it—when she felt Jace nudge her arm.

He held out a plate with a plastic knife and fork resting on top. "Thought I would make this a little easier on me," he said with a crooked grin.

Dodie gave him an answering smile and gladly took the plate. "Thanks. I hadn't figured this would turn into fine dining."

"Remind me to take you out to a really fancy restaurant sometime," Jace said with a grin, as he dumped his fries beside his burger on the plate. Then he lowered his head.

She was about to tease him about inspecting his fries. Then she noticed his eyes were closed—and she realized he was praying.

Guilt stabbed her. The same guilt that assaulted her whenever her mother quizzed her about her church or Bible study attendance.

She used to pray. And read the Bible. And attend Bible study. And try to keep other kids on the straight and narrow.

Fat lot of good that did her.

But she still waited until he lifted his head before she took another bite.

"So, why did you pick burgers by the river instead of salmon at the Inn?" Jace asked, dipping a French fry into a pile of ketchup on his plate.

Dodie shrugged. "I like the ambience here."

"Well, works good for me. Cheap date."

Not a date, she wanted to correct him, but she decided it would be easier to let the comment slide.

"Surely a hotshot lawyer like you doesn't have to worry about money," she teased instead, fishing a pickle from her burger.

"I still have a few debts to pay."

"Student loans?"

"A few. Not as many as I would have if I hadn't gotten the help I did. I'm thankful and humbled by the support I've received so far. Carson has been a tremendous help and encouragement." He gave her a careful smile. "I know you're not crazy about Chuck, but I'm indebted to him. Gave me a place to stay while I studied. Been a listening ear and even helped me get through…some bad times."

Jace stopped there, but Dodie sensed the bad times had much to do with her.

She looked away and picked up a French fry. "So what's next for Jace Scholte?"

"I have some goals that I want to reach."

"Like…" When she and Jace were dating they often talked about the things they wanted to do, the people they wanted to save. They both were on fire with a desire to do justice and to see justice served.

They both had been so naive.

"I want to make my mother proud. I want to make Carson proud that he chose to help me."

"It's evident how much their respect means to you." Dodie kept her voice light as she swirled another fry through a puddle of ketchup on her plate.

"I feel like I owe it to both of them. I know I've been blessed."

"Do you feel God has blessed you, too?" She couldn't help the harsh tone of her voice, but it just came out.

"I believe God has blessed me with brains, health and opportunities, yes. It would be wrong not to use them." Jace slipped his jacket off and rolled up his sleeves, as if shedding his lawyer persona.

Dodie popped the fry in her mouth, hoping she sounded more relaxed than she felt. "You still go to church?"

Jace nodded, tossing her a quick sidelong glance. "I need to go. I have to be reminded that I need God in my life and I need to be in community with other believers." He wiped his mouth and dropped the napkin in the paper bag. "What about you? I notice you don't go very regularly."

She shrugged. "People change."

"You changed a lot, Dodie. You were the one who challenged me." Jace gave her a wry look. "You were the one who told me God would not be mocked. It was because of you I started going to church."

Dodie heard the faintest hint of consternation tingeing his voice, but she couldn't let it slip through her defenses.

"God and I don't see eye to eye anymore." But even as she spoke the words, she felt a twinge of older emotions, of deeper connections with the Lord. At one time she and God had a relationship just as at one time she and Jace had.

But both relationships had been shattered that horrible day, six years ago.

She chanced a quick look at Jace and was agitated when her eyes were drawn into his intense gaze.

She couldn't look away.

"It bothers me that you've turned your back on God. Why is that? Once you loved Him so much." Jace leaned forward, his arms resting on his knees.

She wanted to shrug away his concern, but at the same time she felt an urge to let him see her life from her perspective. If nothing else, he was an old friend, and on that basis he needed to know a bit more than what she had given him.

"I always did the right thing. Pleased the right people—my mom, my friends, my teachers. And then, when things got difficult for me, I decided I was tired of working so hard to be what everyone else wanted me to be. I decided I was going to take a break. Just do things that caught my fancy or my attention."

Jace laughed, but he sounded puzzled. "So working at the coffee shop, the thrift store and the farmer's market were part of that break?"

"I know it sounds very provincial of me, but I enjoyed it at first." Dodie turned her attention back to the last few French fries on her plate. But she wasn't hungry anymore.

"At first," Jace prompted.

Too late she realized her slip. She shouldn't have been surprised that he caught it. He was trained, after all, to catch inconsistencies.

"Any job loses its glow after a while," she conceded. "Even being a lawyer."

"If you could pick your ideal job, what would it be?"

Dodie set her plate aside and wrapped her arms around her knees, staring out over the water as it flowed past her. "I would like to help people. People who are lost. Confused."

A silence followed this small confession, broken only by the murmur of water over rocks.

"I want you to know I've been praying for you," Jace said finally, his voice somber. "Ever since you left law school. Praying you'd be safe. Praying that you'd be okay."

His words created a hungering ache in her chest. She hadn't been able to pray when she took the cab to the airport, when she sat hunched on the airplane staring sightlessly out of the window, feeling violated, afraid and unworthy.

She hadn't been able to pray when she phoned her parents and told them she was in Europe and that she needed money.

Sometimes she wanted to pray, but mostly she preferred to ignore God or, if she felt extra frustrated, throw up an angry tirade at Him.

That wasn't prayer. Prayer was loving communication with God, not curled fists raised at the ceiling of her apartment as fury overtook her.

God would not be mocked, she remembered telling

Jace when he was the one wandering and she seemed to be on the right path. God would not be mocked, but neither would He tolerate her temper tantrums. She was so sure of that, she stopped praying.

But now, for the first time in years, she wanted to give her pain voice. To finally let it out.

"Maybe you should have prayed before," she whispered.

Jace frowned. "Before what?"

She shook her head, mentally backtracking from the dangerous edge she'd been slipping toward.

She hesitated and Jace moved a bit closer, put his hand on her arm.

Dodie didn't even stop to think and covered his hand with hers, letting her fingers slide back and forth over his knuckles. She half turned, and their gazes locked.

"Dodie." Her name came out on a sigh and then Jace reached out his other hand and stroked her cheek and her hair. His fingers trailed gently over her face and then he cupped her face.

And then, incredibly, he leaned closer. His face blurred and as her eyes slid shut she felt his lips touch hers.

The initial contact was so feather-light she might have imagined it, yet her heart thundered its response. She caught him by the shoulder, and then they were in each other's arms, his mouth moving over hers.

It was as if the years had melted away and they were once again Dodie and Jace, young and in love.

Jace pulled back, his expression tender as his eyes scanned her face. "I missed you," he said, his deep and achingly familiar voice washing over her.

"I missed you, too." Her heart stuttered and a lump rose in her throat. She couldn't cry. Not now. Not when things were so fragile.

Jace touched her face again. "What happened, Dodie? What went wrong? Why did you leave?"

His concern tugged at her.

Would he understand?

Would he believe her?

"I was so worried about you. I tried and tried to call you. Even Chuck and Carson helped me try to find you. They were so helpful but we couldn't find anything out."

Her breath knotted in her throat.

Too close. Too close. She couldn't do this.

She pulled away.

"Sorry, Jace. But I gotta go."

"Go where?"

She shook her head. "Doesn't matter. I want to go."

She saw him lift one hand and unconsciously she jerked away. But as soon as she did, she felt foolish. This was Jace. The man who had always been so tender and caring. She was about to apologize but he didn't give her the chance.

"Dodie. No. Please… I wouldn't hurt you." Jace's voice was full of anguish as he lowered his hand. "I'm sorry, it's just…"

The distress in his voice cut her like a knife. But she got up anyway.

Not trusting herself to talk, she began to pack up, tossing the remnants of her food into one of the takeout bags. Jace said nothing as he folded the blanket.

Dodie handed him the plates and utensils and together in silence they walked back to the car.

Jace opened the door for her, and Dodie looked from it to him and then shook her head. "I'd like to walk home."

"That'll take you over an hour," Jace protested. "I brought you here—I'll bring you home."

But after the confusion of emotions she had just gone through, she needed some time alone. Time to think. To sort through what had just happened.

"Please, Jace. I need some space."

Jace put his hand on her arm. Tightened his grip a little, as if to anchor her to him.

"You're not going to run away again, are you?"

She shook her head. "I've nowhere else to go."

"What do you mean?"

Telling him would be such a relief, but as she held his concerned gaze, she thought of what he had always said about Carson. How Carson admired him.

Jace won't believe you, the harsh voice from the past mocked her.

She knew the voice was right.

Chapter Seven

"Coffee. Medium roast. To stay." Jace stood before Dodie and gave his order in a dispassionate voice.

On Monday mornings Dodie worked for Janie, and when Janie's other part-time help came, she moved on to the thrift store for the afternoon. He didn't have the time to spare to come here, but even so he left the pile of work sitting on his office desk and walked down the street to the coffee shop. All in the hope of building on the small advance he'd made with Dodie on their "date."

Dodie filled up a ceramic mug and set it on the counter. When she held her hand out for his money, her gaze slipped upward and he caught the faintest hint of yearning in her eyes.

Since Saturday, he'd been itching to call her. To make sure she was okay. All he could do was pray and trust that the kiss they had shared was the beginning of something. Anything. He had even secretly hoped that she would come to church. But Sunday came and she had stayed away.

"Busy this morning?" he asked, as he handed her his cash.

"No more than usual." She crossed her arms over her chest as a defense mechanism. "By the way, I've got a donation of an original painting by a friend of mine, but I can't pick it up until six tonight. Her stuff usually sells pretty high, so I'm not comfortable leaving it at my apartment overnight." She paused. "Are you working late at the office again?"

Again? Had she noticed?

"Yeah. Sure." If Dodie was coming by he'd be there. He leaned his one elbow on the counter, which brought him a little closer to Dodie. "So, what are your plans for the weekend?"

"Nothing special. Why do you ask?" To his surprise, she moved closer herself.

He waited a moment. "I was wondering if you'd be interested in catching the movie showing at the theater this Friday."

Dodie's withdrawal would not have been noticed by anyone else, but Jace caught it. A slight darkening of her gaze, lips pressed together.

Then, to his surprise, she shrugged. "I heard it was funny."

"Funny is good." He waited. She hadn't said yes, but she hadn't said no, either. The doorbell jangled and another customer came into the shop. Jace reluctantly took his coffee and moved away from the counter. He sat where he could watch Dodie and he noticed, from time to time, that her eyes would slide over to him, then away.

One step at a time, he thought, sipping his coffee and watching her watch him.

She was rinsing an empty coffee jug in the sink when he stood to follow up on the movie invitation.

But then his cell phone rang, and he saw it was Carson calling.

So, instead of asking her out, Jace tossed off a goodbye wave and answered the phone.

"Hello, Carson," he said, as he pulled open the door of the shop. "What can I do for you?"

"Just checking in," Carson said, his gravelly voice resonating across the airwaves. "Heard that you're doing a great job back there in Riverbend."

"Things seem to be coming together both on and off the job," Jace said, striding down the street. Just hearing his boss's voice was enough to make him straighten his back, pick up the pace.

"Yeah, I heard you managed to coax some well-known singer out of retirement to sing at the fundraiser. That's quite a feat. I'm proud of you, son."

Though Carson's admiration warmed Jace's heart, he knew he had to give credit where it was due. "I didn't have much to do with Helen Lennox, I'm afraid. That was all Dodie."

"Is she still involved in the fundraiser?"

Carson sounded surprised, but then if Jace was honest with himself, he had to admit that Dodie's dedication surprised him, as well. Though she won the challenge, she was still finding people to donate items. On Friday she had brought in a hand-knit sweater from an elderly woman who had heard about the fundraiser from a friend of a friend. Now this painting from another one of her contacts.

"Dodie and I had a little contest going to see who could get the most donations and she beat me handily. I had to take her out for dinner as a result."

"Really. Just like old times, eh?"

Not really, Jace thought, remembering the various

emotions that had slipped over Dodie's features—and how their kiss profoundly affected him. Time had changed much for both of them, but to his surprise and dismay, the old attraction had returned so easily he knew it had never left.

"Yeah. Just like old times," he murmured.

"That's good…I suppose."

Jace almost felt the reservations in Carson's voice. "You don't sound thrilled."

Carson's sigh underlined his uncertainty. "I'll be blunt, Jace. You've got a bright future. Riverbend is just a stopover, and from the things I'm hearing about the work you're doing there, you've got some good things waiting for you here in Edmonton."

Jace's heart lurched at the inherent promise in Carson's voice. "I'm glad to hear that," he said, keeping his comment purposely vague.

"You need to keep focused. Keep your eye on the prize, so to speak. Someone like Dodie could, potentially, be a hindrance to you."

Jace frowned, pausing at the corner of the street. A client of his smiled and waved, and he waved back.

"Dodie doesn't have staying power, Jace," Carson continued. "Normally I don't like to interfere in my employee's personal lives, but in your case I feel like I have a stake in your success, and I don't want to see you throw it away."

Jace understood the subtext in Carson's words. Thanks to Carson's financial support Jace had graduated with minimal student debt. Though he had initially felt guilty and had tried to find ways to repay him, Carson kept expressing his gratitude for saving Chuck's life the night of the accident. He kept telling Jace that all he wanted as repayment was a commitment from Jace to work for him.

Which Jace did without hesitation. He and Dodie had both admired and respected Carson and, it seemed, the feeling was mutual. When he, Chuck and Dodie were all offered summer jobs at his law firm, it had seemed like a dream come true instead of an obligation.

Now he was looking at a huge move up the career ladder. His life was definitely on track. He was moving in the direction he had mapped out for himself.

"I truly appreciate the affirmation," Jace said as he pushed open the door of his office. "But I believe you're wrong about Dodie."

He wished he could find the right words to explain to Carson how he felt. Dodie had been a huge part of his life and an integral part of the very success Carson spoke of. Not only had she challenged him to change the course of his life when he and Chuck were palling around in high school, but after that horrific accident, it had been her words ringing through his head as he lay in the hospital. He'd never forget that he was the one who gave him the Bible that he'd found such comfort in.

Although Carson had supplied the financial means, it was Dodie who had inspired him to turn back to God.

That she was on a different path right now had something to do with that summer six years ago, and he was determined to find out what it was. Maybe not this weekend or the next, but eventually he would discover what made her drop out of his life, quit school and travel halfway around the world.

Carson sighed. "I don't think someone like Dodie would be an asset to you. Besides, she's not going to move from Riverbend and those wacky little jobs I hear from Chuck that she's holding down."

Jace understood Carson's frustration. Hadn't he felt exactly the same?

But Jace had known Dodie longer than Carson had, and since he began working on the fundraiser with her, he'd caught flashes of the Dodie he used to know. And it was those glimpses into who she had been and could be that gave him a ray of hope that he would find her again.

Jace stopped at the reception desk and shuffled one-handed through the mail. Callie handed him a couple of phone messages.

"Important?" he mouthed, holding up the messages, meaning did he have to see to them directly.

Callie was about to reply when her phone rang. He waved her off, then put the stack of messages on top of a letter he was waiting for and headed down the hall.

"I gave that girl every chance that you and Chuck got. And she threw it all back in my face when she left without saying anything to me. No words of thanks for the job I'd given her, no explanation. Nothing. I think that should speak to her character," Carson was saying.

Jace felt a riffle of anger at Carson's comment as he pushed open the door to his office. "I don't think Dodie's character is up for debate."

"You're right. I apologize." Carson was quiet a moment, as if giving himself space to move on. "At any rate, I just wanted to touch base with you. I was looking at some of these files. Are you sure you're charging all your time? Because it seems to me that your hours for the Griswold file are a bit thin."

Thanks to the previous lawyer, Jace had spent a lot of extra time rewriting the will that Mr. and Mrs. Griswold had gotten him to draw up. But Jace didn't think Mr. and Mrs. Griswold should be charged for Harvey's mistakes.

"I am billing the way I should."

The moment of silence following his assertion spoke

volumes. Carson was always after him to make sure he billed properly, explaining that the more accurate the hours were, the more equitable the bills.

But now and again Jace couldn't help but think that Carson was trying to eke out whatever he could wherever he could.

He dismissed the thought as ungenerous. Carson was a businessman and he had every right to run his law firm using sound business practices.

Still…

"Just make sure you don't short yourself. I didn't send you out there to do charity work," Carson said with a quick laugh. "If you need anything, let me know. Chuck said he would gladly help out on this end."

"I don't think that's necessary, but I do have something I want to go over with you." Jace picked a file off his desk, and soon he and Carson were going over the legalities of some mistakes Harvey had made on a partnership agreement.

No sooner had he hung up then the phone rang again, and Jace was immersed back in his work.

The day slipped past, and by the time his secretary left, Jace felt as if he had done two days' work in one. He looked up from the computer and blinked at the clock. It was 5:36 p.m. He smiled. Dodie said she was coming by with a painting. He'd have a chance to press her about the movie.

But an hour and a half later, Dodie still hadn't shown up, nor was she answering her cell phone. Jace couldn't help but think about Carson's comment. Was she truly unreliable?

Or was she simply afraid to see him again?

He waited ten more minutes then called her at home, but there was no answer.

He didn't have a chance to follow up on why she hadn't come because the next day he left for Edmonton. He had to catch up on his workload there.

He knew he shouldn't care as much as he did. That didn't stop him from regularly checking his cell phone and his personal e-mail while he was in the city. But there was no message from her.

Was she doing it again?

He tried to ignore that nagging thought.

Did that bother him because her no-show underlined what Carson had hinted about her? Or was it because he felt like she was avoiding him? He had foolishly thought their moment by the river, their shared kiss, had as much of an impact on her as it had on him.

When he returned to Riverbend on Thursday he decided he'd had enough with the uncertainty. He was going to the thrift store and he was just going to ask her, point-blank, what happened.

He strode down the sidewalk, pushed open the door and let his eyes adjust a moment from the bright sun outside.

Dodie stood behind the counter sorting through a bag of clothes. She looked up, and her surprised expression gave Jace a curious lift in spite of his frustration with her.

"So you decided to store the painting at your place?" he asked bluntly. "I waited at the office for quite a while the other night."

Dodie frowned. "I left a message with your secretary. My friend called me right after you left the coffee shop. She told me she would drop the painting off at your office this afternoon."

"Callie didn't say anything to me before she left that day, nor did she give me any message."

"I specifically told her to give you the message." She gave him a quick smile. "Didn't want you to think I was unreliable."

Her unconscious repetition of the very words Carson had used gave him a guilty start.

Then he thought of the scribbled messages his secretary had given that day, the ones Callie had said weren't important. He realized he hadn't even looked at them. One of them had probably been from Dodie.

"No problem." Relief sluiced through him. Thank goodness he hadn't called her. He would have looked like a fool. And behind that came another thought.

Carson had been wrong.

In a much better mood now, he glanced around the shop, surprised at the ambience. Clothes were sorted by kind and size, hanging neatly from circular racks. On top of each waist-high rack stood a mannequin modeling an outfit. The fanciful outfits on each mannequin made Jace guess that Dodie had a hand in dressing them.

Shelves full of toys lined one wall. Another set of shelves held shoes, neatly laid out. It looked like a regular clothing store, except some of the items were obviously used.

"See anything you like?" Dodie asked, a faint edge in her voice.

"I actually might, if I had time to look around." Jace jerked his chin at the piles of clothes. "What are you doing?"

"Triage. We get so many donations that we have to be ruthless about what we keep." Dodie held up a neon pink shirt with a rip down one sleeve and mismatched buttons. "See, this kind of thing?" She tossed it over her shoulder in a colorful arc. "To the dump. No one would buy it."

"People still give a lot of junk, don't they?"

Dodie shook her head. "I don't know why people

don't stop to think what people would be willing to spend money on."

He leaned an elbow on the counter, moving a bit closer to her. He was about to ask her about the movie again and once again they were interrupted.

A young woman with two young children came into the shop. Dodie hurried around the counter, as if eager to escape him.

"Hey, Linda, how are you doing? What do you need today? Something for Krissie?" Dodie squatted down to get on the girl's level. "Do you need a new dress? Or some pants today? Or does your doll need something?" The little girl responded, shyly at first, then gaining enthusiasm and momentum as she talked about her clothes, her doll and then the party she was invited to.

While Jace watched, Dodie's conversation shifted from the mother to the little girl and, occasionally, to the little boy in the stroller.

She was animated and friendly.

And incredibly appealing.

Ten minutes later, as Dodie rang up Linda's purchases, the little girl looked up at Jace, a frown wrinkling her forehead. "Aren't you going to buy anything?" she asked.

"I might," he said. "There's lots to pick from, isn't there?"

"My mommy says this store is a godsend," Krissie said, clutching her doll. "Except I don't know what that means."

Jace couldn't help a quick glance at her mother's older-style coat and worn blue jeans. He knew exactly what it meant. He, his sister and mother had often come to a store quite similar this one. Only then the thrift shop was in a dingy store down a back alley and someone like Dodie wasn't sorting the donations, weeding out the junk.

That was the job of the shopper. It took many dedicated

hours of sifting through torn and stained clothes to find something suitable in order to save a few precious dollars.

As the family left with their purchases, Jace felt a rush of appreciation and, yes, gratitude that this woman didn't have to do the same. He was glad she had a welcoming and cheerful store to shop in and that people like Dodie had done much of the legwork already.

Dodie may deny her faith in God, Jace thought, may say she didn't believe in Him anymore, but he realized she was doing what God required. Doing justice, performing loving kindnesses and walking humbly with God, even though she might not realize that was where she was going.

And in that moment, he allowed himself to hope she would return to her faith.

And, maybe, return to him.

Dodie went back to her sorting, intent on deciding whether a pair of lace-trimmed jeans would make the cut.

Jace leaned an elbow on the counter, watching her. He could tell, however, that she was as aware of him as he was of her. Every now and then her eyes would slide to him and a faint flush would color her cheeks.

He clenched his fists to keep himself from brushing his knuckle over her cheeks.

And as he looked at her lips, he too easily remembered their shared kiss.

"So, is there something else you want?" she asked, finally. "I don't want to be getting in the way of your career."

"My career is doing okay right about now," he said with a grin. "Chuck is going to have to watch his back when I get back to Edmonton."

"Chuck was always good at that," Dodie snapped.

Dodie had never cared for Chuck and had always said

that Carson was too easy on him. Often Jace agreed, but he didn't want to talk about Chuck.

"Sounds like things are coming together for the fundraiser," he said, sensing a change of topics was in order. "Only a couple of weeks now."

"I've got most of my stuff in."

"And then some." Jace released a theatrical sigh. "Bad enough you beat me, now you seem to want to rub my nose in it by bringing stuff in again and again."

"I'm competitive by nature."

"I remember that from school," he said with a laugh. "Always a fight for me to get better marks than you."

"I liked beating you," she said, returning his smile.

"Do you ever think of going back to school?"

She held his gaze and it was as if her eyes pierced into his soul. "I know you saw those textbooks on my coffee table."

He held his hand up. "Guilty as charged."

"But to satisfy your rapacious curiosity, yes, I do think of going back to school and have been taking courses toward that."

"Counseling?"

"I know it's not in the same league as charging corporate clients their left eye to set up their accounts, draft contracts and evade taxes, but it's important."

Jace ran his thumbnail along a scratch in the counter, wishing he didn't feel so defensive. "Is that how you see what I do?"

"Sorry—that wasn't fair. I know what you do is important…it's just… People had other plans for my life and I didn't agree with them."

Jace's mind ticked back to other conversations with Dodie while they were in college. Conversations about family expectations and personal duty. "People like your mother?"

Dodie nodded. "I know she loves me and all that, but I also know that she's had me pegged for some type of degree since my fourth-grade teacher recommended that I skip a grade. And then, when I was elected valedictorian in high school, she set her sights on lawyer. She's had plans for me."

"And those plans didn't include working in a thrift store or helping Janie out or selling stuff at the farmer's market?"

Dodie snorted. "Most definitely not."

Jace glanced around the store. "I have to confess, your current career choices are a surprise for me, too." He thought of what they had talked about on their "date" by the river. What she said made sense, but he still had the feeling that something was missing from the equation. Dodie moving so dramatically from prelaw to thrift store still didn't add up in his mind.

"Confess away. It's good for the soul," Dodie quipped.

The phone on the counter rang and Jace felt a spark of irritation. He had better get to the point soon. He had shunned his work for too long, and he had to get back to it. But not before he asked her out again.

"I suppose I could find someone to pick them up."

Jace glanced at Dodie. Her forehead was puckered in a frown.

"I could talk to Ethan," she was saying, referring to her cousin. "Maybe he'd lend me that beloved truck of his." She bit her lip. "I'll give you a call when I can find out more." Her frown deepened after she hung up the phone.

"Something wrong?"

Dodie looked distracted. "Arnie DeVries, the man who makes the chairs, wants me to pick them up on Sunday.

He's leaving for Arizona on Monday morning and won't be back before the fundraiser. But I need a truck." She picked up the phone again.

"I have a truck," Jace offered, thankful once again that his mother hadn't sold his father's truck like he had urged her to.

Dodie looked from him to the phone. Her indecision wasn't encouraging. When she picked up the phone, Jace against fought back frustration. He was about to push himself away from the counter when she put the phone back on the hook and gave him a tentative smile.

"Thanks for the offer. I'll take you up on it."

"I'd better drive, though. The truck is dependable, but temperamental." He waited a moment, then she nodded. "When do you need to pick this up?"

"He asked me to come at about twelve-thirty, which means we'd have to leave my place at about eleven-thirty." Then Dodie hesitated. "Church is over at eleven-thirty, right?"

He nodded. "And it would take me at least fifteen minutes to get from church to your place."

"I suppose I could meet you at church," she said.

"Or you could come to church. That way we won't miss each other." Jace threw out the comment with a casual air, as if it didn't matter as much as it did.

"I guess I could. I haven't been in a while. Mom and Dad would be pleased."

"So, see you Sunday, then?"

"Yeah. Sure."

Though her comment was affirmative, it wasn't enthusiastic, and Jace wondered if she was really going to follow through.

Chapter Eight

Dodie parked her car down the street from the church, turned off the engine and wondered, yet again, what she was doing.

It was Jace's fault, she thought. Jace with his praying at their picnic. Jace with his comment about a part of her needing God.

Last night, she pulled her Bible out of the cupboard for the first time in years. She had taken it to bed, laid it on the bedside table, like she used to.

But she hadn't been able to open it. Not yet.

She wasn't ready for a one-on-one conversation with God. But church she could manage. Once in a while she attended to keep her father happy and her mother off her back. This would be no different.

Dodie stepped out of the car and strode down the sidewalk, heading for the front doors of the building. Once inside, she glanced around, her gaze skimming over the people milling in the foyer. She gave a smile to a friend, dodged a little girl who was squealing at her sister to wait up for her. If she could find Janie, she would sit with her.

Or, barring that, one of her cousins.

Then, just as she was about to head up the stairs to the sanctuary, a deep voice called her name, and a shiver raced down her spine.

Jace stood behind her. Today he wore a crisp blue shirt, with a corduroy blazer, denim jeans and cowboy boots.

Dodie felt a faint trill of attraction. Her Jace, she thought.

"Good to see you here," Jace said, rolling up the bulletin he'd received from the ushers at the door.

"Good to be here." Dodie inclined her head but as she moved up the stairs, she sensed Jace right behind her.

Dodie scanned the pews from the back of the church. She saw Sarah and Logan, but there was no room beside them. Ditto Ethan and a very pregnant Hannah.

Janie and Luke weren't here yet.

There was room by her mother, but Dodie didn't feel like dealing with the surprise she knew her mother would show.

But could she really sit by herself?

"Can I sit with you?" Jace asked casually. "I hardly know anyone here and I hate sitting alone."

Dodie chuckled, then nodded. "Sure. Why not?" She led the way to a spot not too close to the front, but not so far from the back that it looked like she was trying to hide.

They settled into the pew. Dodie buried herself in the bulletin, catching up on the news of the coming week.

A notice for the fundraiser was on the front. Helen Lennox's name was printed in bold letters.

I am a part of this, Dodie thought with a sense of pride. The rest of the bulletin was filled with information about other regular events—youth group, Bible study groups for every age; a fun night was scheduled for girls seven to twelve. Another notice gave progress on some of the people in the congregation who were ill.

So familiar, Dodie thought, as she glanced around the church that she had attended since she was a baby. She had seen fellow classmates leave for other places, then return, get married and settle down. Three of her high school classmates now lived here, all three of them married, all three of them with children.

Panic flickered through her at the idea that she was getting left behind. In a couple of weeks she would be turning thirty. What had she really accomplished in her life?

She couldn't help a quick, sidelong glance at Jace, sitting beside her. He was reading the bulletin, a light frown puckering his brow. He always did that when he was reading, she thought, the memory like a gentle ache.

She turned her attention back to the bulletin, frustrated with the emotions that flittered through her soul.

You made your own choices, the annoying inner voice reminded her.

Choices that were forced upon me, she told herself. I didn't ask to be assaulted. To have my sense of self-worth stripped away from me.

Dodie slammed the door on the wayward thoughts. She couldn't indulge in any sense of self-pity. She was on her own and she simply had to deal. Just like she had for the past six years.

The music started, signaling the beginning of the worship service. Dodie looked up at the overhead, recognizing the song as an old favorite of hers that she hadn't heard in a long time.

She easily fell into the rhythm of the service after the pastor's welcome and the responses.

She was glad she came, she thought as she sat down, getting ready for the sermon. This was comfortingly familiar. And she knew it would make her parents happy.

A smile played at her lips. And anything that made her parents happy kept her mother off her back.

"I'd like us all to turn to Psalm 16." The pastor's announcement was followed by a rustling of pages. Out of the corner of her eye, Dodie saw Jace pull the Bible out of the holder in the pew. He turned to the passage and, just as he used to when they were dating, held it open so both of them could read it.

Dodie could have looked aside and Jace would not have been the wiser, but a gentle yearning drew her eyes to the passage.

"Keep me safe, O God, for in you I take refuge. I said to the Lord, You are my Lord; apart from You I have no good thing."

The familiar cadence and rhythm called back memories of herself as a young girl. At one time she had tried to memorize all the Psalms, thinking that the Lord would be pleased with her devotion.

And now, as the pastor's voice spoke aloud words that were at one time imprinted on her mind, she heard them as if for the first time.

"Apart from you I have no good thing."

She had tried to stay apart from God and keep Him at arm's length. But the emptiness percolating into her life seemed to be harder to ignore and stave off.

Now she was sitting in church with Jace beside her. Just like she used to six years ago.

Six years. The words clutched at her heart and she drew a shuddering breath as the intervening years of loneliness and heartache seeped into her mind.

For years she had kept God at arm's length. The God she used to take comfort from, strength from and peace from.

He had let her down.

But what had her life become since she had pushed God away? Had her life been joyful? Had she found contentment? The Psalm seemed to mock that spiritual independence. Seemed to declare that her life had become empty and void of the one thing that gave her meaning.

"We yearn for justice," the pastor was saying. "We yearn for the good things God gives us. Augustine says that our hearts are restless until they find our rest in God."

The pastor's sermon dove deep into Dodie's soul. He was speaking her thoughts, raising them up from the dark places she had assigned them after that life-altering night, when she'd been trying not to believe that she had "asked for" what had happened to her.

This was why you stay away from church. To keep God out of your life. The God who didn't protect you. The God who didn't keep you safe.

She closed her eyes against a wave of old pain and anger and shame. She didn't know if she was ready to let God into her life. Ready to make herself vulnerable again. Ready to face, fully, what had happened to her. Ready to let the people who meant so much to her find out.

She didn't know if she could confront the shame and, yes, the guilt. Because no matter how much self-talk she had indulged in, always lurking in the back of her mind was the notion that she had asked for what had happened to her.

As her attacker had told her.

"Are you okay?"

Jace's whispered question sifted into her sorrow and as she glanced up at his familiar face, better memories rose to the surface. Memories of how his arm felt over her shoulder, the feel of her hand twined in his, how Janie would tease her about how close she sat to Jace. She studied him again, seeing the changes wrought by the intervening years.

Unfamiliar lines faintly fanned out from the corners of his eyes. His face had grown an unfamiliar hardness around his mouth. The suits he usually wore spoke of money spent, money that had become important to Jace.

He was moving down another path than they had planned. The Jace sitting beside her wanted bigger things, more money, success.

Yet he was still Jace. And when his eyes met hers, she realized that he could still resurrect the same feelings in her.

She felt a measure of fear and, below that, a curious sense of expectancy. As if something was going to happen.

She wasn't sure what it would be. Or if she would be able to welcome it.

But when Jace smiled at her, for a brief moment, she thought she might.

"Yeah. I'm fine." But her voice wobbled on the words, and to her shame his face grew shimmery as moisture pooled in her eyes. Would he understand if she told him everything?

She turned away, but not before catching his light frown. She swallowed once, then again, as a fresh wave of sorrow came over her. Then she felt Jace's hand resting lightly on her shoulder.

She blinked and tears slid down her cheeks. She didn't move to brush them away, hoping Jace wouldn't notice.

Then his hand tightened, and she knew he had.

She drew a steadying breath, suddenly thankful for his support and thankful for his nearness. She had missed him so much, she realized, as she slipped her hand into his and curled her fingers around his hand.

They sat this way until the pastor announced the

closing song and Dodie reluctantly got to her feet. When the pastor pronounced the blessing she chanced another look at Jace. Her heart leapt when she saw the emotion on his face.

It was as if the years had been swept away.

He still cares about me, she thought.

And on the heels of that thought came one just as earth-shattering:

I still care for him.

"This is beautiful work," Jace said, running his hand over the smooth wood of the chair.

The chair was made of hundreds of small pieces of wood laminated together and then painstakingly shaped and sanded.

"Of course it is," muttered Arnie. "I don't make junk."

Dodie looked over at the chair's creator. His dark brown hair was streaked with grey and liberally flecked with sawdust. He hadn't cracked a smile since Dodie and Jace had come onto his yard, which wasn't unusual. Arnie was as generous with his smiles as he was with his chairs.

Dodie turned to Jace. "You should try out the chair. It's so comfortable."

Thankfully Arnie couldn't see Jace's skeptical look.

"Sit in it," Dodie urged.

Arnie sucked on his pipe, then waved it at the chair. "Try it, mister. Guaranteed you won't find anything as well-made in any of your fancy city stores."

Dodie was surprised at the flare of irritation flashing across Jace's face. Did it matter to him that Arnie DeVries saw him, a one-time inhabitant of Riverbend, as an urban dweller?

"Sure. I'll try it."

When he sat down, Dodie could see from the look on his face that he was surprised himself at how comfortable it was. "This is amazing," he remarked.

Perfect. Just the reaction she was hoping for. She knew if Jace complimented Arnie, the man would soften toward him.

She didn't want to analyze too deeply why it mattered to her that Arnie saw Jace as a city lawyer.

"I could sit in this chair for a long time," Jace said. "It's really comfortable."

"It's the loving care that goes into the making of the chair that makes it so comfy," Dodie said with a touch of irony in her voice.

She saw Jace bite back a laugh as he glanced from her to Arnie leaning against his workbench, his pipe clamped between his teeth, his eyes glaring at Jace from the leathery folds of his face.

It always surprised Dodie that something so beautiful could come from someone as antisocial as Arnie was.

Dodie turned to him. "This is fantastic. I really appreciate your generosity in donating this."

He shrugged Dodie's thanks aside. "Just make sure you take care loading it. Get a dent in it, it will lose value."

"Or gain some character," Dodie teased. "But we will be very careful with it and treat it with the respect it deserves. It's not every day we get to handle an Arnie DeVries chair." She flashed a smile at him.

A wreath of smoke surrounded Arnie's face, but Dodie saw the beginnings of a reluctant smile tug at the man's mouth as he pushed himself away from the bench.

Jace got up from the chair and stood back as Arnie wrapped the chair in a couple of old blankets. "I want these back," he said, as he tied a couple of lengths of knotted rope around the chair. "I'll need them for the next chair."

"I'll make sure I get them back to you as soon as possible," Dodie said, flashing him another charming smile.

Fifteen minutes later, after helping Arnie secure the chair to his satisfaction, Dodie and Jace were driving off the yard. Dodie leaned out the window, waved to Arnie, then pulled her head back in the truck and buckled up.

"So. Now you've met one of Riverbend's resident artistes." Dodie chuckled as she rolled up the window.

"He's certainly a character," Jace said with a grin.

"But you have to admit, he makes beautiful stuff. I'm pretty tickled that he was willing to donate one of his chairs. He usually only sells them to people after he's done a thorough background check." Dodie sat back in the truck with a heady sense of satisfaction.

"Yet he seemed pretty happy to give one to you."

"Arnie would never admit it, but he owes me."

"How so?"

"I saved him from a casserole widow. She was coming on to him and Paul every Saturday at the farmer's market. I convinced the woman that Arnie was still pining for a long-lost love and how hard it would be for the widow to capture his heart."

"I take it the long-lost love didn't exist?"

"Not that he's ever told me, but I drew on my own vast experience and managed to convince her."

Jace glanced her way. "Your own *vast* experience?"

Her heart flopped over in her chest at his emphasis. Had she really said that? Was he thinking she'd been pining for him?

Dodie flapped her hand at Jace in an effort to make him think otherwise. "I was being sarcastic. I mean, it's not like I've spent a lot of time pining for you…or anyone else, for that matter—"

Stop, stop before you stumble into a minefield you can't retreat from.

But in spite of her desire to keep the past in the past, memories slipped in.

She and Jace driving to the lookout point where they would sit and talk.

And kiss.

Like the kiss they had shared at the river. Dodie swallowed as past melded into present.

Needing a distraction, she turned on the radio. "Does this thing work?"

"No. Sorry."

She sat back, tapping her fingers on her arm as a few more miles slipped by. Then Jace slowed the truck by a road that veered left, and a premonition fingered its way down her spine.

"This is the way to the lookout point, isn't it?" Jace asked.

"Yeah. But we usually came at it from the other way."

He turned to her. "Do you mind if we check it out? I haven't been here in ages. I'd love to see what the river valley looks like now that the trees are leafed out."

Dodie gave him a casual shrug, wondering if he'd been able to read her mind. "Fine by me."

Jace flashed her a thankful grin, then spun the steering wheel and turned onto the road.

"You do realize we're trespassing on Logan Carleton's land," Dodie said.

"If he catches us I'll say it was your idea." Jace gripped the wheel as the truck bumped and jolted over the tree-lined road that was little more than a rough path, exactly the width of a truck.

"I believe you used that excuse before. Just shortly before he did catch us."

"But now he's married to your cousin Sarah. And that makes everything okay." Jace tapped his forehead as he grinned at her. "See how my keen legal mind is always working?"

"Your keen legal mind better keep its focus on the road," Dodie grunted, as the truck bounced over a deep rut. "I don't want to get any scratches or marks on that chair in the back."

"Sorry." Jace grabbed the wheel and righted the truck. After a few more bone-jarring bumps and turns so tight that branches scraped along the sides of the truck, they broke out into an open area.

Jace stopped the truck, turned it off and got out. Dodie hesitated a moment but then followed suit.

Below them, the sparkling river spooled away in either direction. A hawk circled lazily over the field below them, and Dodie heard the muted chatter of wild swans coming from the riverbank.

She hugged herself, letting the peace and silence of the place wash over her.

"I missed this," Jace said, his hands resting on his hips as he glanced over the valley. Jace sighed lightly, then, to Dodie's surprise, sat down on the grass.

She wasn't sure what to do, but it looked like he was going to stay awhile. So she eased herself down beside him. Not too close, yet not too far away, either.

Jace plucked a dry piece of grass left over from last fall and twirled it around between his fingers. The afternoon sun warmed Dodie's neck, offsetting the cool breeze wafting up from the river.

"Do you ever come out here?" Jace asked.

His question was quiet, but Dodie sensed that he was asking if she made any forays into the past. If she missed what they had shared enough to remind herself.

She shook her head. "I've never had any reason to."

He said nothing, simply twirling the grass around and around.

"We'll have to spend the day of the fundraiser putting the auction items out," Jace said after a while, thankfully moving the conversation to the events currently binding them together. "Will you be able to spare the time?"

"I'm sure I can get the day off." Dodie fiddled with the zipper pull on her cardigan. "I also spoke to Helen yesterday," she continued. "Just to make sure things were still okay on her end. She's a bit nervous but looking forward to it."

Jace rested his arms on his elbows. "I can't tell you what a windfall that was, getting her on board. You never did tell me how you managed."

"Not sure myself. That night that we went to their place, when you and Paul were outside, we talked."

"I know that she had a rough childhood and supposedly a bad marriage. Did she say anything about that?"

"Just that she thought the counseling program and the center was something she wished she'd had access to growing up." Dodie thought of the pain she saw in Helen's eyes. A pain that was frighteningly familiar.

For a moment, sitting across from Helen as she doled out small parts of her past, Dodie felt as if Helen was a kindred spirit. As if she, of all people, might understand.

But shyness in the presence of such a well-known singer, and six years of suppression, kept her own secrets locked up.

"She did say that the center was one of the reasons she wanted to help out. I didn't have to do much convincing," Dodie added.

Jace nodded. "When we were talking, I sensed that she was a woman who had suffered deep pain."

Jace's quiet words sent a shiver down her spine. "How did you know?" she asked.

"Just a feeling I had." Jace held Dodie's gaze for an extra beat as if probing for her own pain.

Dodie wanted to look away, but felt herself drawn into his gaze.

Can I tell him everything?

Her heart stepped up its erratic rhythm as words fought to be spoken.

Then he gave her an enigmatic smile, looked back at the river and the moment passed. "Well, I'm glad she is involved," Jace said, "The tickets are just about sold out."

Dodie drew in a long, steadying breath. She had been so close to telling Jace what had happened to her that horrible night. She choked it down. She couldn't. It was too shameful. Too horrible.

He wouldn't understand. And if she saw him turn away from her, it would devastate her. Far better that she make that choice and not him.

"Is the speaker still not feeling well?" she asked, thankful that her voice was so steady.

"Last I heard, there wasn't much improvement."

"What will you do if he can't come?"

Jace shrugged his shoulders. "We tried to contact some of the backup people we had in mind, but they're also booked. So far, our only line of defense is prayer."

His word hung between them, a reminder of the differences between them.

"Good thing you still have faith."

A faint smile curved his lips. "Trusting in God has gotten me through some rough times in the past. And praying helps me build my relationship with the Lord."

"Has God answered all your prayers? Is that why you're doing so well?" As soon as she asked the question she regretted giving it voice. She was striking out, blindly trying to keep him from probing into her own life.

"I know how I got to where I am," Jace said, but he seemed a bit uncomfortable at her question. "I believe I've been blessed, but I also know that I worked hard. Using what God has given me to get to where I am. And I'm going to keep working until I get to where I want to be."

"And where's that?"

Jace gently twirled the grass between his fingers. "Partner in Carson's law firm."

Dodie wondered why he wouldn't meet her gaze. "You don't sound completely convinced."

Jace sighed and raised one eyebrow, which, in turn, pulled up the scar that ran along the side of his face.

Dodie remembered tracing that scar with her finger. After the accident he'd been self-conscious about it, but Dodie had told him that combined with his dark hair and blue eyes, the scar gave him an air of brooding mystique. Now she had to twine her fingers around each other to keep from reaching across the slight distance between them.

"Sometimes I feel like I'm doing exactly what I want to do. But I would be lying if I didn't say there are times I have my doubts." He lifted his shoulder in a vague shrug. "I like the challenge and I like the paycheck."

Dodie felt a tinge of regret. "I guess at the end of the day, that has value."

"Lots if I become partner." Jace flashed her a wry smile. "But you sound disappointed."

"Money isn't everything, Jace Scholte."

"That's easy to say when you've grown up with it."

"Maybe, but it does give me another perspective on it. I love my parents, but I don't think they were any happier than yours were." She had visited Jace's parents numerous times while they dated and had always enjoyed going to their home. It always seemed more welcoming and cozy than the house she grew up in.

"Really?" Jace sent a dubious look her way. "You never got to hear the fights I did. And most of them were over money."

"News flash, Jace. My parents fought over money, too," Dodie snapped.

"Not the same way mine did. Your parents could buy whatever they wanted."

"Correction. They could buy whatever *you* wanted. Trust me, my parents had a whole different set of wants, just as unattainable and just as much fuel for fights."

He shot her a surprised look, but this time she held his gaze.

"You sound like Dodie again. Arguing and haranguing me into your point of view." Jace leaned back, grinning at her. "The world lost a talented lawyer when you quit law school." He was quiet a moment. "Would you ever go back? To law school?"

Dodie hugged her knees, letting the thought settle. Her mother had asked her a couple of times, and Dodie had always managed to joke her way out of answering. Janie had wondered, as well, but thankfully had left things be.

Now Jace was asking her.

Then she shook her head. "I don't think so. I don't have

any desire to put myself through that stress and pressure. I did it because my mom seemed to think this was something I should pursue, and since they were footing the bill I figured I should listen." She stopped there, unwilling to tell him that he was the other reason she pursued law. It was something they could do together. "I know that it seems like a waste of my education, not to use it—"

"But you're building on that now," Jace said. "With the courses you're taking."

"That's true," she conceded.

"What made you want to pursue counseling?"

Dodie edged around the words to formulate her reasons. "I think it's something that has purpose and meaning. I like that I can help people."

She let her eyes drift over to Jace. His expression was thoughtful as he watched her.

"You wanted to be a lawyer for the same reason," he said. "I'm glad to see that part of you is still alive and well."

Dodie wanted to shrug off his comment, but their shared history made her feel she should expand on his comment. "There are a lot of parts of me still alive and well."

Jace's smile seemed to agree. "And your relationship with God?"

"God is alive and well. As for how we get along…" Dodie let the sentence trail off, her own doubts assailing her. "I've given up on trying to satisfy Him. I decided to simply go my own way."

Then Jace touched her shoulder, creating a gentle intimacy. "I'm not going to lie. I really want to know why you pulled away from God, from me, but I don't want to preach. So tell me about the course you're taking."

To her surprise she felt a momentary pang of regret at the change in subject and at the withdrawal of his hand.

Talking with Jace had created a faint stirring in her soul. As if a distant voice called her name, drawing her back to a place she once felt safe, secure and loved.

"I'm enjoying it and, surprise, doing quite well."

Jace angled her a curious smile. "I'm not surprised."

"Well, my mother is."

Jace held her gaze, his smile slipping away. "Is that still important to you?"

Dodie blinked, then leaned back, as well, the palms of her hands resting on the old, dry grass. "It shouldn't be," she admitted. "Goodness knows I've tried hard enough to show her I'm my own person."

"Maybe a bit too hard?"

"Maybe," she admitted. "Mom's never been that easy to please, so I guess it wouldn't matter how hard I tried or didn't."

"I think her opinion has always been too important to you."

Dodie shrugged, not looking at him.

"How much longer is the course?" he continued.

"I can do another few classes by correspondence, then I need to do a practicum and take one semester in school in Edmonton."

"Edmonton?" He quirked an eyebrow at her. "Would you consider moving to the city again?"

Dodie shook her head. "I like it here—Riverbend's my home. I feel safe here."

"Safe?"

Dodie pressed her lips together, regretting the slip. Trust Jace to pick up on it.

She felt his hand on her neck before she even realized he had moved closer to her. His fingers teased at her hair, toying with it.

"Do you feel safe with me?" he asked.

Dodie tested the question a moment, then granted him a smile. "Yes, I do."

Jace's only reply was to move his hand, to trace the line of her eyebrows and then her lips. "I'm not going to push you, to ask you what happened in the past. But I want you to know that I missed you so much."

Her heart began a shallow rhythm and she took a fluttering breath.

"Did you miss me?" he asked, his voice no louder than the breeze whispering past them.

She could only nod.

A gentle smile drifted over his lips. "I'm glad to know that. I always wondered…"

"Jace…I'm sorry…" She wanted to say so much more, but her throat closed off.

"I'm glad you are. I'm sorry, too." His eyes skimmed her face and came to rest on hers. "There's a lot of water under the bridge, so to speak. But maybe we don't need to go back. Maybe we can start right here."

Dodie caught his hand in hers, hope fluttering in her chest. "What do you mean?"

"Can we keep things simple? Can we just be Dodie and Jace? Here and now?"

Dodie felt a heady rush of joy and gratitude press against her chest.

"No questions asked," he continued. "No looking back. Just now."

She turned her head and pressed her lips against his hand. Just like she used to.

"I think I can do that," she whispered.

"We don't have to look back or try to fix what happened.

We could just be together. I know we're meant to be together. I feel it."

"I feel the same way." And she did. She had missed him so terribly those first few months. Even though she was the one who had stayed away, she didn't do it out of choice, she reminded herself.

His smile created a welcoming warmth in her soul.

He drew her close and once again their lips met. Once again they were connected on so many levels.

Dodie clung to him, feeling a happiness she hadn't felt in years.

Just here. Just now.

She repeated the words to secure them in her mind.

She wouldn't have to lay open the shame that dogged her the past few years. She could leave it in the past and truly move on. She could be with Jace. And if the painful memories resurfaced, she would do what she had always done. Push it back where it belonged. She wouldn't need to deal with it at all.

And maybe, just maybe, he would be willing to stay here in Riverbend.

Chapter Nine

"Heard you and Jace went to the lookout point." Janie said, wringing out a cloth in the sink and then wiping down the coffee machines.

Dodie shoved the mop in the pail and shot her sister an annoyed look. It was on the tip of her tongue to tell Janie to mind her own business, but she knew that wouldn't stop her sister. If anything it would pique her curiosity.

"So where are things going with you two anyhow?" Janie continued.

"Where they should be." Dodie wrung out the mop. "One day at a time."

"With a detour to the lookout point."

"We're old friends. He wanted to talk. That's all." She wasn't going to mention the kiss. Her sister didn't need to know everything.

"And you sat in church together."

Dodie heard the faint condemnation in her sister's voice and felt a sliver of apprehension.

"It just worked out that way." Dodie wiped up the water

she had slopped over the floor, then dropped the mop back in the pail. "Anything else you want me to do?"

Janie looked at Dodie. "You're not telling me everything, sister."

"What's to tell? You seem to know every little bit of my life as it is."

"So what changed between you and Jace? Once upon a time you couldn't even tolerate hearing his name, now you're spending time with him."

"Just because of the fundraiser. That's all." Dodie wheeled the pail back to the storage room. But when she returned, Janie was leaning against the counter.

"You know I love you, Dodie."

"I'm not talking about Jace." Dodie grabbed her jacket off the chair and stuffed her arms in the sleeves. She wasn't ready to explore the tentative place she and Jace had come to. It wasn't perfect but, considering their past, for now it was a good thing.

"I know you two used to date. I know that at one time you were pretty serious," Janie continued, determined to give Dodie advice whether she wanted it or not.

"And I know that you've never been crazy about him," Dodie retorted. "And I'm sure you have your reasons, but Jace is a good person."

"Jace has his own agenda, Dodie. Always has. And I wouldn't be a good sister if I didn't warn you to be cautious. You know he's going back to that high-powered city job of his. He's not going to be staying in Riverbend."

Dodie looked at her sister's expression of concern and self-doubt skittered across her mind.

"Maybe, maybe not," she said with an edge in her voice.

"You think you can convince him to stay here? Jace has never had any love for Riverbend. You know that."

She did, but maybe, since he started working here and since he started working on the fundraiser, his opinion had changed. Riverbend was a good place and she did not want to consider him going back to the city.

Going back to Carson MacGregor's law firm.

Then her cell phone rang, jolting her into reality.

It was Jace.

"Hey. What can I do for you?" she said, turning away from Janie and the disapproval she saw in her eyes.

"Hey, did you get a call from Sheila?"

"What about?"

"She just called. Said we were supposed to get together tonight to put together the catalog."

Dodie mentally scrambled over her agenda. "This is news to me."

"Can you come? She said she couldn't come tomorrow night, and there's no way I'm going if you're not there."

"Are you afraid?" Dodie smiled, relieved that in spite of the emotions roiling around her insides, she could still tease him.

"Well, yeah. I'd rather not be alone with her."

"I'm at Janie's right now. I'll be right there." She flipped her phone closed. "Sorry, Janie. I have to run. Fundraising stuff."

"So that means you'll see Jace again," Janie said with a frown.

"And Sheila," Dodie reminded her.

She didn't need to have any of her own self-doubts voiced. One small part of her hoped, in the tiniest way, that he would change his mind. That he would stay.

But that was for another time.

For now it was simple, she reminded herself. Just her and Jace and the now.

She flung her purse over her shoulder, walked out the door and hurried down the street.

Sheila was leaning against her car when Dodie approached Jace's office. She wore snug, faded blue jeans tucked into leather boots, and a revealing T-shirt.

"What are you doing here?" she asked with a frown, pushing herself away from her vehicle.

"Jace just called me," Dodie said. "Reminded me of the meeting."

"You didn't need to come," Sheila said, a slightly snippy tone in her voice.

"I don't want you to have to do all the work. That wouldn't be fair." Dodie gave her a smile that wasn't returned.

A few minutes later, Jace parked his car beside Sheila's. As he walked toward them, his gaze caught and held Dodie's.

She couldn't help her reaction to the look in his eyes and his slow smile. "Hey there," he murmured.

"Hey, yourself."

"Shall we get at it," Sheila snapped, as she pulled her laptop out of her car. "I have other things to do."

"Of course you do." Jace gave Dodie a wink, pulled the keys out of his pocket and let them in the front door.

Sheila went in first and stalked down the hallway, clutching her laptop, her hair swinging with every step.

Jace caught Dodie by the arm and gave her a light tug.

"Thanks for coming on such short notice," he whispered. "You saved my life. I hope you didn't have any other plans."

Dodie gave him a quick smile. "No plans and no problem" was all she said, feeling suddenly shy around him. In spite of their shared history, she felt as if they were starting from a different place.

She hoped it was a better place.

They entered the room just as Sheila was setting up her laptop. "Let's get started," she said, frowning at her computer screen. "We should first do up the cards that will go with each item as we catalog them. Dodie, why don't you start with the stuff in the other room?"

Sheila handed Dodie a stack of papers on a clipboard, a pen and a large envelope, and gave her detailed instructions on how to label and track each item.

"I'll help her," Jace said, heading out the door ahead of Dodie.

He rolled his eyes as he closed the door on Sheila's murmured protest.

"I think she likes you." Dodie allowed herself a teasing smile as she opened the door to the other room and turned on the light.

Jace closed the door behind her, then turned her around, placed his hands on her shoulder and gently kissed her. "Now my day is much better."

Dodie let her eyes follow the contours of his face and traced the scar that ran down his cheek.

"My day is better, too," she said quietly, smiling into his eyes.

"Really?"

"Really."

Jace stroked her hair back from her face. "I missed you."

"I missed you, too," she whispered.

Jace looked like he was about to kiss her again and she pressed her hand to his chest. She wasn't going to be rushed.

"We better get going if we don't want Sheila to come here and find out what's going on."

"I think she should find out what's going on," Jace said with a hint of anger in his voice. "But you're right." He traced the line of her eyebrow, and smiled again, his anger gone. "Besides, I promised I would take things slow."

Dodie opened the envelope that Sheila had given her and glanced around the room. "So, which item should be number 0001?"

Jace held up a coffee mug. "Ladies and gentlemen, we have a winner."

Dodie laughed and in minutes they fell into an easy rhythm, joking about some of the items, admiring others.

As they worked in close proximity, Dodie grew more aware of Jace. But at the same time, she grew more confident.

This was going to work, she thought, stealing a quick glance at him. They could truly start over. Square one. Fresh beginnings.

She could put the past behind her.

"I just remembered. Helen phoned," Jace said. "She wanted some information on the fundraiser. She said she tried to contact you."

"Oh!" Dodie realized with a start. "I left my cell phone in my car." She looked over at him. "What did she have to say?"

"We were supposed to meet with Helen and I thought we could reschedule for Friday at her place," Jace continued. "After the fundraising meeting."

Dodie's mind went utterly blank. Oh, brother. She was scatterbrained today. She hadn't checked her calendar this morning. "Sure. Sounds good."

Jace shot her a frown. "Don't tell me you've forgotten about the fundraising meeting as well?"

She didn't like the emphasis on the, *as well.*

"I have it written down," Dodie said in her own defense. Jace held her gaze as if trying to figure out what happened to the girl who used to remember everything. The girl who used to be depended on to be told something once and be able to remember every detail a few months later.

That girl is gone, she wanted to tell him again. *I no longer want to be that girl who was so determined to be everything to everybody.*

A quick knock on the door gave her a start. Sheila poked her head into the room, her eyes flitting from Dodie to Jace. "I'm getting a coffee. Anyone want one?"

They both shook their heads and Sheila gave a tight nod. "Okay, I'll be back in a bit," she said, disappointment lacing her voice.

"What are we going to discuss at the meeting?" Dodie asked after Sheila left, thankful that she hadn't interrupted them any sooner.

"I got a call from the fundraiser chairman. The speaker we had booked for the fundraiser officially canceled."

Dodie clutched the quilt she had been refolding. "That's terrible news."

"I know. We're working on some of our backup speakers, but that's not looking too good, either. Do you think Helen might be convinced to do a longer set?"

Dodie shrugged. "Might be worth asking. She seemed open to the whole idea in the first place."

Jace smiled. "I was hoping you'd say that."

He glanced out the window beside the door of the office, then stole a quick kiss.

Dodie's heart fluttered double time at the casualness of his touch.

He's kissed you before, she chastised herself. But this felt different. Time had moved them to this tentative place.

And what are you going to do when he talks about going back to the city?

Dodie banished the questions that had the potential to ruin her good mood. She and Jace were together right now…and that was enough, she reminded herself. The future could wait.

She shot a quick look Jace's way as she carefully labeled the quilt. "You don't seem very upset about what's happening with the fundraiser."

"I am, but I never thought we needed a speaker, especially once Helen got on board. The evening was full enough. If Helen is willing to expand her set list, I think people would sooner hear her than a speaker." He leaned back against the table, his eyes snapping with suppressed enthusiasm. "The other reason I'm not too upset is that I got a call from Carson just before you came here. He's offered me a huge case."

She frowned as a sense of unease feathered through her. "But what about your work here?"

Jace frowned. "This was always just a temporary stay. You knew that."

She did, but ever since their time at the lookout point, she had harbored the faint hope that he might consider it to be more permanent.

He's never going to stay.

Janie's words were like a premonition now.

Jace caught her by the hands and smiled. "You were thinking I would stay, weren't you?"

Dodie gave him a negligent shrug. "Yeah. Just a bit."

"But you know that me working for Carson has always been the plan. From the first time we dated."

Dodie didn't reply. She didn't want to get into a fight over this. Not when things were just starting to gel between them.

"Tell me about the case," she said instead, moving to safer territory.

Jace grinned with barely suppressed excitement. "Remember the news story a couple of weeks back? The one with the high-profile businessman?"

"The oil guy?" Dodie struggled to keep her composure. She remembered seeing the case on television. Remembered seeing that Carson was going to defend him, though she was sketchy on the details.

Her hands trembled as she smoothed them over the quilt.

"Carson wants me on the team as cocounsel."

Dodie swallowed, as a shadow edged into her mind.

"There is only one problem. He wants me to come back to Edmonton right after the fundraiser."

Dodie struggled to marshal her thoughts, not sure which one to process first.

Jace working on a case with Carson. Jace moving to the city much sooner.

"I know it's sudden, and it's sooner than I had thought, but this is such a huge chance for me. Carson has already found someone to replace me here so I'm free to go as soon as possible." Jace squeezed her hands a bit harder as his eyes lit up. "I owe Carson so much, and this is a chance to repay him and advance my career."

"I think that your debt to Carson has been long paid," Dodie snapped, struggling to maintain her composure as memories battered her crumbling defenses. "What's the guy been charged with, anyway?"

Jace sighed. "Carson is convinced the guy is innocent, but he's been charged with rape—"

Jace's mouth kept moving, but Dodie heard nothing past the roaring in her ears. Then the room spun around and she clutched Jace's hands to keep her balance.

Only one word resounded in her mind.

No.

"Dodie. Are you okay?" Jace eased her back into a chair. "You look white as a sheet. What's wrong?" He held her hands even more tightly, his frown showing his concern.

"You're helping Carson MacGregor defend a rapist?"

"Alleged, Dodie. You know yourself that a man is innocent until proven guilty."

"You can't do this."

"What are you saying?" he asked.

"You have to call him back. Tell him you can't do this. It's impossible. You can't work with Carson like that." Dodie clamped her lips together, ice slipping through her veins.

"What's going on, Dodie? What are you talking about?"

She couldn't breathe anymore.

She closed her eyes, dredging up the anger that had sustained her so many times during the past six years.

Since her own rape.

"Is this about me going back to Edmonton? You knew that was going to happen. I thought you were okay with that." He paused for a long moment and then locked eyes with her. "I thought you might consider moving back with me. You had talked about going back to finish your counseling courses—"

Dodie's heart pounded while Jace spoke. She laid the quilt down with deliberate movements as she tried to plan her next move.

Jace was so obviously proud that he'd gotten on this case.

She slowly chose her next words. "If you take this case, then I can't be with you."

"What? You can't be serious. This is what criminal law is all about. You know that."

Dodie was surprised she could keep her voice so steady even as the blood rushed through her head, making everything inside of her a whirling mass of fear. She swallowed as she walked toward the door on unsteady feet.

But Jace stood in front of her and he wasn't moving. "You would really walk away from me because of this case?"

"Please, let me get out of here."

Jace dragged his hand over his face, as if trying to arrange his thoughts. And while he was distracted, Dodie yanked the door open, intent on only one thing. Escape. She couldn't breathe.

I just need to get away, she told herself. *To think. To recoup.*

"Dodie. Come back here," Jace called out from behind her. "Tell me what's wrong."

I'm such a fool, she thought. *I knew Jace worked for Carson. How in the world did I think I could keep our worlds separate?*

"Just leave me alone, Jace. I need to be alone."

She burst out of Jace's office and into the street. The sun still shone, she thought with a measure of surprise as she strode down the sidewalk. She didn't even glance back to see if Jace was following her. She had one focus.

Get home. Get safe.

"Where is Dodie?" Helen asked on Friday as she held the door open to let Jace into the warmth of her home.

Jace wanted to cover for Dodie's absence and make up some excuse. But the reality was he had been doing a slow burn for the past couple of days.

He had stayed away from Janie's coffee shop yesterday. There was no way he was going to look like he was chasing her down.

And then, this evening at the hall, when the chairman

of the fundraiser called the meeting to order and Dodie still hadn't shown up, Jace had gotten really angry.

She hadn't been bluffing. She was staying away from him over a case that had the potential to change his career. To get him everything he wanted even sooner than he had expected.

"I was looking forward to seeing her again," Helen said, her voice full of regret as they walked to the living room. "She's an interesting person."

Jace pulled his thoughts to the present. "Dodie goes her own way," he said, unable to keep the resentful tone out of his voice.

He felt like he was dealing with a myriad of emotions. Anger that he'd been shut out of her life again and confusion as to why.

She knew he was going back to Edmonton. Knew that his goal was to work his way up in Carson's law firm. Why was she so upset that he was following through on this? Did she think he was going to stay around in Riverbend, stuck in the same town his parents had been? The town that didn't hold many good memories for him?

But even as he formulated the thought, he remembered some of the comments people had made about his father. How respected he was in the community. How, in spite of his disability, he was involved in many functions and events.

He didn't remember any of that. All he could remember was the lack of money. His mother's dissatisfaction.

Helen sank down into her chair, leaning back, her arms wrapped around her midsection. "Paul said she was a bit of a free spirit."

Free spirit is maybe putting it more kindly than I would have, Jace thought, as he sat down across from Helen. But then, he had known Dodie as someone who could be depended on. Someone who stuck things out until the end.

He glanced around the room. "Paul isn't here, either?"

"He's out feeding the chickens and goats and getting inspiration for the next song he wants to write. He'll join us soon."

Jace pulled a notebook out of the briefcase he had brought with him and leaned back in his chair. "Paul said you wanted to go over the set list for the fundraiser."

Helen cocked her head to one side, her hair falling away from her face, revealing the lines around her mouth, the fan of wrinkles bracketing her eyes. "I take it you don't want to talk about Dodie anymore."

Jace wasn't sure how to respond to this direct comment so he simply shook his head. "Preferably not."

"I'm being forward because I sensed, the last time you two were here, that something was going on between you. In fact, I was quite sure you were dating, but Paul said it wasn't so."

Jace wasn't sure what to do with this direction of the conversation. Wasn't sure how much to say, but his frustration had worn away his usual guard. "Dodie and I had dated at one time," he admitted. "But that was many years ago."

"What happened?"

Jace blew out his breath as he tapped his pen on the notebook. Then he looked up at Helen. "I don't know. She never told me."

Helen rocked back and forth in her chair, her eyes focused in the distance. "Have you asked?"

"Many times." He pressed his lips together. His emotions were getting the better of him.

"How long were you two dating?"

"It started in high school. We went to prom together."

"High school sweethearts," Helen said with a gentle smile. "What came after high school?"

"College, then law school. We grew more and more serious. In fact, I had been saving up for an engagement ring."

"Why did you break up?"

Jace leaned back and crossed his arms, his mind sifting back in time. "We didn't. We'd been working together for the man I'm working for now. We were doing a summer internship at Carson's law office. One night she was working late and the next day, when we were supposed to meet each other, she didn't show." Jace stopped there. Helen didn't need a complete rundown of his and Dodie's love life. Or lack thereof.

"And…" Helen prompted.

Jace held her steady gaze and shook his head. "Why do you care?"

Helen's eyes slipped away as she looked past him, but Jace sensed she was looking beyond this space and time.

"Because I see in her eyes a deep and aching pain. A pain that I know all too well."

Her words gave him a chill and for a moment, he couldn't say anything.

"Why do you say that?"

Helen waited a moment then turned to him. "I don't want to presume to sound as if I know more than you do about someone you know better than me." She let a faint smile tease her lips. "But when I talked to her, after you and Paul left, I got a strong sense that she and I have traveled the same path."

"How can you say that? Her parents were well off. She had everything. A good life, faith. She never had to scrimp and scrape like you did. Like I did."

"Like you did…?" she prompted.

"My parents never had a lot of money. We were always scrambling to pay even the smallest bills. My sister and I have been hungry, and I've faced ridicule because of the place I lived, my secondhand clothes." He stopped, surprised at what he was telling this woman, a virtual stranger.

"'My first shoes were worn by you first…'" Helen smiled as she quoted a line from one of the songs she wrote. "I know what you're talking about. Public humiliation, especially in front of your peers, is a difficult thing to face." A shadow crossed her face. "But Dodie's pain comes from a far deeper place. A place that can't be fixed in spite of how well off you've perceived her family to be."

"But where is this place? What caused this pain? She won't tell me anything. All I know is that all those years ago she suddenly left town, left me." Jace leaned forward. "Now she's doing it again. She's shutting me out and not telling me why. She's not answering her phone, not calling me."

Helen sat back, watching him. Jace held her gaze, as if hoping for some words of wisdom from her. Anything that would help him to get through to Dodie.

"You still care for her, don't you?"

Jace sighed, shaking his head, as if ashamed of his own stupidity. "Yes. Fool that I am…still do."

"Not a fool, Jace. Never a fool for caring for somebody. Because I think she cares for you, too. She just doesn't know what to do with it."

"How do you know all this?"

"Like I said, I sensed a kindred spirit when I talked to her. A kindred sorrow. And I know that the way Paul got to me was to keep caring. To put away his own pride and let his affection wear away my resistance and mistrust of men." Helen stopped, then gave him a careful smile. "I could go on and on, but I'm guessing you are a man with other things on his mind, so let's talk about the other reason you came here."

She leaned back in her chair. "I'll need to make a trip to the venue and do a sound check. I like to have my ducks in a row before I perform...."

Jace was thankful for the switch of topics, but Helen had given him much to think about.

Later, he thought, putting the information aside. He couldn't assimilate it all now. He had to think about this later.

"We've had a problem with our speaker," Jace said, handing her a temporary agenda. "We're not sure how we're going to fill that space, and the only way this will affect you is that you might be singing sooner in the program."

Helen skimmed over the program. "You'll actually have quite a full evening with the live and silent auctions and me singing, so it might not be so bad not to have the speaker." She tapped her finger on her cheek, as if thinking. "If you want, I could add a few more songs. I know something that had always gone over well in my concerts was when I explained, to the audience, how some of the songs came about."

Jace hardly dared to believe she would be willing to do that. To him, it was enough that she was singing. Now this?

"If you don't mind—"

"I wouldn't offer if I minded. I'm glad to help out. This is a good cause and I'm now part of the community." She gave him a wistful smile. "I haven't been a part of community for a long time and I think it's important to help where you can."

"So you think community is important."

She looked him in the eye. "Very important. You and

Dodie are very fortunate to have been born and raised here. To have history and continuity. And I'm very thankful Paul brought me here. To this town." She glanced at the clock and got up. "Paul will be in soon. Would you like to stay and have some tea with us?"

Jace nodded and, as Helen bustled about the kitchen, he thought of her comments.

He had spent a lot of time and energy trying to get away from the very place she seemed quite content to settle in. The first time he'd been here, he focused on his work, on moving on. He had virtually no social life.

Now, thanks to being involved in the fundraiser, he'd seen parts of his parents' lives through other people's eyes and from a different vantage point. They were well respected in spite of their lack of money. They were involved in the town and people remembered them.

He thought about Dodie's veiled comments about him being ashamed of the community he was born and raised in. It wasn't the community—it was his parents.

And it turned out he had nothing to be ashamed of.

He glanced over at Helen, thinking once again what she said.

Dodie was a kindred spirit and they shared a kindred sorrow.

But what sorrow could that be?

He did know one thing, though. This time he wasn't going to try to phone her. He was going to go to her apartment and confront her.

And he wasn't going to leave until he got answers to all his questions.

Chapter Ten

Helen's voice rang through the speakers of Dodie's stereo. She didn't care how loud she played her music. Right now she needed other words to drown out the ones replaying in her head since Jace dropped his bomb a few days ago.

She wrapped her arms around her legs as she hunched on the couch, letting Helen's words speak for her.

"Pain without ceasing, shame without end. Pain that won't leave, shame that won't bend."

She knows exactly what happened to me, Dodie thought, laying her head on her knees. She understands what no one else can.

The phone rang again and Dodie glanced at the handset sitting beside her on the couch.

Unknown name. Unknown number.

No one she needed to talk to.

Dodie had phoned Janie yesterday to tell her she wasn't feeling well and wouldn't be coming in again that day. She'd called her mother back last night, just to reassure her that, yes, she was still alive and she would feel better in a while.

I'm going to be working with Carson MacGregor on a rape case.

He didn't know, but at the same time, the thought sent an arrow through her midsection.

Through the music she heard someone knocking at the door.

"Dodie. Open up. I need to talk to you."

Dodie's heart plunged.

Not Jace. Not now.

"I know you're in there," he said, raising his voice. "I can hear the music and your car is still out in the parking lot."

Dodie gnawed on her lower lip. If she let him in, there would be a confrontation. Jace would not leave without some kind of explanation as to why she took off on him and as to why she'd been avoiding him again.

She didn't want to confront him, so she laid her head on her knees, wishing she could ignore the inevitability of seeing Jace again.

"I'm not leaving and I'm not going to stop knocking until you open the door," he called.

"Hey, be quiet," someone yelled down the hallway. "Some of us are trying to sleep."

"See, Dodie. I'm just going to end up annoying your neighbors," Jace bellowed above the music. "And it will be your fault."

Dodie clung to the faint hope that he would get the hint and leave her alone. Just as he had the last time.

"Shut up down there or I'm coming up there." Another voice joined in the fray, but this one came from downstairs.

Dodie pushed herself off the couch, trudged to the door and took a moment to take a peek through the peephole.

Jace stood in the hallway, wearing a faded denim shirt, a leather jacket, blue jeans, his arms crossed. He was also ignoring the man leaning out the door down the hallway yelling at both of them.

With a sense of impending doom, Dodie opened the deadbolt, unlatched the chain, unlocked the door and opened it just a bit.

"Just leave me alone," she said through the narrow opening she had allowed, clinging to anger, the only defense she had against him.

Jace slowly shook his head. "I've done that too much in the past and I'm not going to do that again."

"Shut that music off, will ya?" This from the man down the hall who now stood in the hallway. Downstairs she heard a door slam against the wall.

"You should probably let me in," Jace suggested, with a lift of his eyebrow.

Dodie saw a shadow in the stairwell, shivered a moment, then quickly unlatched the door. She stood aside as Jace strode into her apartment.

As she closed the door, she felt the room shrink. He seemed to fill up the space with his presence.

"You're listening to Helen Lennox?" Jace asked, tilting his head toward the stereo.

"Seemed appropriate." Dodie picked up the remote and hit the Off switch. Silence reigned. She wrapped her arms around herself and walked over to the couch, sinking down onto it. "So, what do you want?"

Jace dropped into a wooden chair across from her, boring his eyes into hers.

Dodie felt a sense of foreboding, but she resisted the temptation to look away. Don't back down, she commanded herself.

"I had planned a dozen of times what I was going to say," he said. "But I always ended up going in circles because I don't even know what I'm supposed to be asking you. I don't even know what to say. I feel like I'm trying to defend myself and I don't even know what I'm accused of."

He stopped and the quiet that rose between them felt thick with old questions and bittersweet memories.

"I thought things had changed in the past few days. I was willing to leave the past in the past." He shoved his hand through his neatly combed hair in a gesture of frustration. "Then, all of a sudden, you're on the run again. I was angry at you when you left me at the office—when you left me to talk to Helen alone."

Dodie's eyes flew to the date on her calendar. Printed in large letters were Helen's name and the time.

Jace followed the direction of her gaze.

"You knew about the meeting," he said.

"I couldn't go."

"Because I was going to be there."

Dodie nodded a tight yes.

"I had an interesting conversation with Helen. She said something that I haven't been able to forget. She said that she sensed you were dealing with a deep pain." Jace's voice grew quiet but Dodie sensed determination in his tone. "What do think she meant?"

Dodie's breath caught in her throat. "I'm not sure," she said. "She probably is just imagining things. She's had her own troubles. I'm sure she is kind of sensitive."

She was babbling, desperately trying to shore up her defenses.

"I thought we were getting somewhere again," he said, his voice vibrating with anger. "I thought we were getting to a point where we could trust each other."

As Dodie's gaze rested on his mouth, she thought of

the time they had spent together and the kisses they had shared. "I'm sorry, Jace." She stifled a surge of regret as she thought of the possibilities she had entertained for a few wonderful days. Possibilities of her and Jace. How foolish she was to think she could keep the past behind her; to keep Carson separate from her life when he was so entwined with Jace's.

Jace pushed himself off the chair and stalked to the window. "I'm a criminal lawyer. I'm going to be taking on some extreme cases." He then turned to her. "So why is this such a problem? Why has this become the line in the sand for you?"

His words were like particles of salt grinding into an opening wound. She wanted to answer him, but the words, so long held down, were lodged in her throat.

"You were drifting before you got on board with this fundraiser, Dodie," Jace continued. "Just meandering along. I know you got involved to satisfy your mother." He crouched down in front of her, looking up into her eyes, as if to make sure she couldn't avoid him anymore. "But then, when you got involved, when you really got behind this, I got to see not only the Dodie I knew, but another side of you. Someone who deeply cares about the people in this community." His tone softened and Dodie began trembling. "Please don't start drifting again."

If he had stayed angry, it would have been so much easier to resist him. If he raised his voice again, like he had just a few moments ago.

Then, when he reached up and ran his finger along her cheek, a sob grew in her throat.

"Dodie, please tell me what is going on. What happened to you?"

You and Carson are going to defend a rapist, she wanted to say.

And she just couldn't.

She pushed his hand aside. "Doesn't matter, Jace. That was a long time ago and it was in the past. You and me, this is never going to work, and we may as well realize it."

"What do you mean, never—"

She sliced her hand through the air, as if to cut off his comment. "You want to live in the city and move up the corporate ladder. I want to stay here. In Riverbend. It's not going to work."

She had to keep her anger up. Keep her emotions high. Because if she didn't, he would find out and that she couldn't bear.

Jace just glared at her. "I don't believe you."

"You'll have to. As long as you're willing to work with Carson on a case like that—" she began.

"I told you—I'm a criminal lawyer. You used to want to be one yourself, before you started drifting along. And now you want to stay in this place and I want to move on."

Dodie held his gaze and then she saw his features soften.

"I really thought things were starting to come together for us," he said. "I thought we had come to a good place."

She had thought so, too. For a few heady days she had honestly thought they could start over. But there were too many barriers between them. And when he told her that he was willing to work with Carson to defend a rapist, she knew that she could never tell him.

She knew he would never believe her. Just as he—her rapist—had told her.

And once again his voice echoed in her mind: *It's your word against mine, missy. And who do you think they're going to believe?*

She willed away the sound of that voice, the shame of that evening. "You better leave, Jace," she said, a hard note entering her voice.

"Why?"

"Because this…us…like I said, it's not going to work."

"You don't want to make it work, do you?" Jace replied, his voice rising again. "Because it's much easier to keep floating along, doing nothing, than it is to make something of yourself."

He moved closer and for a moment fear slithered in her belly.

"You're not telling me everything, Dodie. I can't believe you're willing to give up on us, just because of what I am and what I do."

She held his angry gaze and the wisp of a thought teased her. *Tell him. Tell him everything.*

But even as the thought tantalized, she knew she couldn't. The shame that had dogged her all these years was still too strong.

And she cared too much for Jace to see rejection on his face.

"It's over, Jace," she said, clinging to what little pride she had left. "It was fun while it lasted, but it's over."

A voice in her head cried out, why are you doing this?

But she fought it down. This was how it had to be. She had to keep him away from her or she was going to fall apart.

"You're not going to try, are you?"

She feigned an indifferent shrug. "I don't want to invest anymore in this. Please leave." She clung to her anger, fanning its flames. "Have fun in Edmonton and enjoy your climb up the ladder." She turned away from him, struggling to maintain her composure. "Just go. Now."

Before I fall apart, she added silently.

There was a pause, then the door to her apartment opened and shut behind Jace.

The sound was like a knife to her heart.

Chapter Eleven

He's gone.

The thought made Dodie choke back a sob.

You could have told him, but you sent him away.

He wouldn't have believed me.

You told him to leave.

Only because I was scared to see the rejection in his eyes. Too see the disbelief when I told him about the rape.

And who did it.

Dodie wandered back to the couch, turned on the light beside it then sat down. She felt utterly, totally alone.

You're not alone.

The still, quiet voice whispered into her consciousness and Dodie waited, letting it settle.

You're not alone.

Dodie glanced at the end table where she'd put her Bible the other day. The day after she'd come back from talking to Helen Lennox.

Dodie reached for the Bible and set it on her lap, fingering the gold-stamped words on the front. Then she flipped it open. She randomly searched through it, waiting for something to come out at her and catch her eye.

Finally she turned back to Psalm 16, the one the pastor had read the Sunday she had gone to church.

"Keep me safe O God. For in You I take refuge," Dodie whispered, keeping at bay the silence and the darkness. She read on and when she came to the end, her voice grew. "You will not abandon me to the grave, nor will You let your Holy One see decay."

Dodie felt the strength of these words sustain and comfort her. And yet, she felt a stirring of anger and sorrow. God had not, as the Psalm had said, made her lot secure. The boundary lines of her life had not fallen in pleasant places.

She had been violated, as a woman, in one of the worst possible ways. She had lost her innocence, her trust and her self-respect.

And all of that had caused her to lose the one man she had cared the most for.

She closed the Bible, wishing she could be as sure about the promises it held as she used to be. She got up, pacing through her apartment, restless and afraid.

"Why did you let that happen to me, Lord?" she cried out finally. "That man ruined my life. He robbed me of something I valued. He broke me."

The words echoed through the apartment, and for a moment Dodie wondered if she had done something horribly wrong, raging at God like that. Then she realized, she didn't care.

"You abandoned me. You made me go through that…horrible…horrible…" Her voice broke as she clenched her fists and shook them heavenward. "Why? What had I done wrong? I did everything you asked. I did all the right things."

Dodie felt impotent in her anger and didn't know where to turn. She hauled the pillows off the couch and threw them over her shoulder. She yanked books off her computer desk and tossed them around the room.

She snatched pictures off the wall.

She grabbed the chair Jace had been sitting in and knocked it over.

Surely He took up our infirmities and carried our sorrows. Yet we considered him stricken by God.

Dodie stopped in the middle of the living room, fighting back tears, just as she heard the door of her apartment open.

Her heart plunged down a mine shaft and she spun around, ice splintering through her veins. She hadn't locked the door. Someone was coming in.

"Hey, Dodie. What's up?"

The light from the hallway shadowed the person standing there. But Dodie's heart settled when she recognized who it was.

Janie turned on the light of the main room, then frowned as her eyes took in the state of Dodie's living room.

"Honey, what happened here?"

Dodie's chest was heaving with anger, rage, and a sorrow so deep she hadn't even begun to release it.

Janie stepped over the toppled chair and caught Dodie by the arms. She gently led her to the couch and sat down.

"Your hands are like ice. What's going on? Did someone break in?"

Dodie looked at her sister, as if trying to place her in the upheaval that had just gone on. Then reason entered her life again as she looked around the wreckage of her apartment.

"No. No one broke in."

"So what happened?"

"Give me a minute." Dodie breathed in and out, willing

her erratic heartbeat to settle as she closed the door on the memories. "Jace and I had a fight."

Janie gripped Dodie's shoulders, her eyes flicking over her face, her hands pushing Dodie's hair back as if checking for injuries.

"No. He didn't do any of this," Dodie said, jerking her head back, looking away from her prying eyes. "It was all me. I just…lost my temper."

"You're not trying to cover up for him, are you?"

"No. Janie. Really." Dodie got up and snatched up a pillow from the floor and fluffed it up. She clutched it a moment, gathering her scattered emotions, then laid it on one end of the couch. "I did all this after he left."

"Are you sure?"

Dodie felt a flicker of anger and focused on it, fanning into a righteous flame. "You don't have to make it sound like Jace is some kind of closet abuser. I know you've never cared for him, but he would never, ever hurt me." Her words came out with extra vehemence, underscored by the emotional roller coaster she had just been on.

She then faced her sister, her tears dry now. "He's a good guy, you know."

Janie met her eyes, then looked over the mess in the apartment. "What was the fight about?"

"He's going back to the city." Even as she spoke the words, they sounded unconvincing. Jace's return to the city wasn't a surprise. She had to try harder.

"But…you knew that."

"Well, yeah. But lately he made it sound as if he might stay. And I thought he was going to. But no, Carson calls and he jumps."

"Again, no surprise here."

"Like I said, I thought he was going to stay. I honestly

thought things were going somewhere with us. I thought… after all this time…"

Jane sat down on the couch with a heavy sigh. "I'm sorry, hon, but I could have told you this was going to happen."

Dodie lifted her shoulders in a vague shrug. "Yeah, well…live and learn I guess."

Janie picked up one of the cushions and fingered the edge. "I know you don't want to talk about it, but is that why you took off for Europe that one summer? Because you and Jace had a fight?"

Dodie felt her throat tighten. She swallowed and turned away as she shook her head, trying to find her footing, trying to find an argument her sister would buy to explain her trashing her own apartment. "It wasn't Jace—it was me. I couldn't stand the pressure of law school and felt the walls closing in. It seemed like everyone wanted something from me and I just couldn't deliver anymore. So I left before I had a nervous breakdown." Dodie drew in a steadying breath, pulling herself back to the place she had been before Jace had returned. "I wanted to rethink my life. To rethink what I wanted. To stop being the girl that everyone thought I should be."

Because that hadn't done her any good.

"And lately, I've been feeling the same expectations from Jace, from Mom…from everyone. And tonight, I just lost it."

"Oh, honey, you could have told us." Janie caught Dodie by the shoulders and turned her around. "We knew something was wrong, we just never realized that you were feeling so much pressure."

Dodie felt a flush of guilt, but reminded herself that much of what she was saying was true.

Janie gave Dodie a hug. "I never knew, sister. You should have said something."

Dodie allowed herself a moment of weakness. Of letting her sister comfort her.

"I didn't want to go through all that. I was scared Mom would want me to see a counselor and make me see a doctor." Dodie shrugged. "I got it through then, I'll get through it now. Jace didn't understand, and we fought."

Janie held her gaze, as if trying to peer past the haze of words Dodie was spinning between them.

It's all the truth, Dodie reminded herself again.

"So now, this is who I am," Dodie said. "Being alone is my choice."

"Jace isn't the only man for you, you know," Janie said, making an intuitive leap in her own logic.

Dodie closed her eyes, feeling the sting of tears. At least now, she could feel authentic in her sorrow. "But I really cared for him. I really thought…" Her voice faded away and she swallowed.

"You'll find someone else, you know. You are an amazing and wonderful woman. You're pure and lovely and beautiful. And if Jace can't see that, then he doesn't deserve you."

Janie waited, as if to let this information sink in. Then she picked up Dodie's Bible. "You've been reading this again."

Dodie nodded. "I was reading what the pastor read from the Bible that Sunday I was in church. But I couldn't get past the part about the boundaries of my life falling in pleasant places." She gave a short laugh. "They haven't been so pleasant."

Janie hesitated, then flipped through the Bible, the thin pages rustling in the quiet. "Maybe you need to look at something that more adequately speaks to the pain you're dealing with." She handed the open Bible back to Dodie. "Read some of these passages. They might make a bit more sense."

Dodie glanced down, recognizing the Psalms. The ones she often skipped because she never felt the angry imprecations against justice for enemies ever applied to her. "The cursing Psalms," she said quietly. "How can I find any comfort in that?"

"It's not about comfort. I think God invites honest emotion, He invites interaction. An entire book of the Bible is devoted to lamenting, something we don't pay enough attention to. Something we avoid."

Dodie skimmed the passages, seeing David's anger, his frustration. She sensed a kinship with the words. "I guess, like David, I felt like God had let me down."

"I felt that way toward God when I was married to Owen and then after, when he died. And, as you said, David felt the same way. So you're not alone." Janie took the Bible from Dodie, put a bookmark in the Bible and laid it aside. "Some of this you'll have to deal with—just you and God. I want to challenge you to take some time to pray. To talk to God honestly and tell Him what you're trying to deal with."

Dodie tested the idea as hints of the old relationship she had with God broke in from the edges of her life. At one time, she'd had a relationship. At one time, her prayers had sustained and helped her.

However, her life apart from God had been empty. Lifeless. She'd been trying to outrun Him, but it seemed He was relentless.

Janie must have sensed her hesitation. "Do you want me to pray with you now?"

She lowered her head and nodded. "Sure. Can't hurt."

Janie grasped her sister's hands and squeezed. "Dear Lord, my little sister has been hurting a long time. You know exactly how she feels and You hurt with her. Help her to give her pain over to You. Give her comfort and let her know that she is Your beloved child."

Janie paused and Dodie let the words rest in her mind. Even though Janie didn't know everything, she had said exactly the words Dodie needed to hear.

Beloved child. She was God's beloved child.

"Help us, her family, to understand and to support her," Janie continued. "Be with her and love her. Amen."

Dodie felt like a fraud, but at the same time, her sister's prayer gave her some measure of comfort.

She raised her head and granted her sister a careful smile.

"Thanks, Janie," she said.

Janie touched Dodie's cheek. "I know things haven't been that great for you, but you know, tomorrow things will seem much better."

"Thanks for coming by," Dodie said. "Why did you stop over?"

"I actually just came to borrow your pink skirt…"

"Sure. I'll go get it." Dodie got up, thankful for the return to the ordinary things of life.

She stepped over the fallen chair and by the time she found the skirt and had returned, Janie had cleaned up the living room a bit.

Janie took the skirt and as she folded it over her arm, she gave Dodie a tentative smile. "And don't worry about Jace. If he doesn't come around, he doesn't deserve you."

"Thanks for the advice," Dodie said, walking her sister to the door.

She closed the door behind her and fell back against it, dropping her head into her hands.

She should have told Janie.

But a secret held for six years wasn't easily let go of.

Maybe she would someday. When Jace was gone.

She closed her eyes against the pain those simple words caused her. Jace. Gone.

She had to keep going. She had to be strong. Jace was no longer in her life. Their fight had seen to that.

He couldn't be in Riverbend.

So come Sunday, Jace headed to the city. He even sat with Carson and his wife in church, thankful that something in his life seemed to be normal. He and Carson talked briefly about the case. When Jace returned to Riverbend, it was with renewed purpose. He was a criminal lawyer and he was doing the right thing. And this coming weekend, as soon as the fundraiser was over, he was leaving.

He dove into his work, getting ready for the lawyer that was going to be taking his place and trying to eradicate his fight with Dodie from his mind.

He avoided Janie's coffee shop for three days. And then one day, he pushed himself away from his desk and walked down the street. He wasn't going to let Dodie determine the course of his life anymore. He wasn't going to avoid her like some lovestruck young man. He had some pride, after all.

But when he got to the coffee shop, only Janie stood behind the counter.

The look she gave him wasn't too encouraging.

"What will you have?" she asked, her features composed into an expressionless mask.

"Coffee. To go," he said, glancing around the store, wondering where Dodie was.

"She's not here," Janie said, pouring him his coffee and snapping a lid on with extra force.

Jace nodded, handing Janie a bill and reaching for his coffee.

But Janie kept her hand on the cup, her eyes on his. "I heard you had a fight Saturday night."

Jace should have known her sister would have found out about it so soon. "Can't see how that's any of your business."

Janie sent him a piercing glare. "At any rate, Dodie is hurting right now and she needs some space."

"As you can see, I've been giving her lots of it," Jace returned. He was getting tired of Janie, as well. "I just hope she decides to show up at the fundraiser."

"She'll be there." Janie sighed. "Though I can't see why. She just went along with the whole thing because of Mom. And, she wouldn't admit it anymore, but I think a bit of it was because of you."

Jace's heart lurched. "What do you mean?"

Janie tapped her fingers on her arm. "She's never really gotten over you."

Janie's comment hung between them, full of implications.

"What do you mean?" he said again.

"She's always had a thing for you." The faintest hint of derision entered Janie's voice. "Even after she came back from Europe…I know she still cared for you, though I could never figure out why."

Jace held the first part of her comment to himself, promising to examine it more later. For now, he zeroed in on the last part.

"You never liked me, did you?"

Janie shrugged. "No secret there."

"Why?"

Janie pursed her lips. "You wasted so much of your life," she said. "You could have done so much better in school. You had good parents and family but you always acted like they were a pain in your neck."

Jace clenched his jaw, realizing that, to a point, she was right.

"Dodie is so family-oriented," Janie continued. "So bound to the community she grew up in. She would have stayed in Riverbend if she could. But you didn't like Riverbend. Still don't. You didn't appreciate this town, or your parents. You were so eager to get out of here, so quick to move to the city and set your sights upward. And she cared enough to follow you there."

He bristled at her accusations. "Dodie didn't have to follow me."

"No, but she was willing to make some pretty big sacrifices for you," Janie said. "I always wondered what sacrifices you would have made for her."

Jace held Janie's gaze, feeling the challenge in it and, at the same time, wishing he didn't care so much about what Janie was saying. "You say she needs space and I've tried to give it to her, but I didn't exactly quit thinking about her when she left me high and dry. She mattered a lot to me. Still does." That last was a concession to the feelings he couldn't seem to sweep away, no matter how often he went over the fight he and Dodie had.

Then he saw a begrudging smile slip across Janie's mouth. "I'll tell her you stopped by."

And that was it. She turned away and Jace stood there a moment, holding his cup of coffee. He took a sip.

Cold.

Then he set the cup on the counter and walked out. His replacement was coming tomorrow and he had to get ready for him. And then he had to get ready to move back to Edmonton.

And what about Dodie?

He wished he knew the answer to that. Because even if he went to the city, he wasn't so sure he could completely put her behind him.

Chapter Twelve

Happy Birthday to me, Dodie thought as she smoothed her hand over her soft green dress, adjusted the high, beaded neckline. She should have let Janie throw her a birthday party. Celebrating thirty years of life and still single was preferable to facing Jace at the fundraiser tonight.

You can stay home.

The pernicious voice returned but Dodie banished it. She had spent the day at home and ignored the phone, knowing the calls would be from her family wishing her a happy birthday. She felt anything but happy.

She took another look at herself in the mirror. She had argued back and forth with herself for the past hour. Stay. Go. Stay. Go.

Her head was tired. She had to follow through on this. She still felt she had to prove to Jace that she was the kind of person who stuck with things to the end.

She didn't want to be defeated by what happened to her. After the fundraiser Jace was leaving, and then she could get back to her life the way it was before he invaded it.

Someday she would tell her family what happened.

But not yet. Not with Jace so close. Once he was out of her life for good, she could release her secrets and finally move on.

She carefully tucked a wayward strand of hair back up, pressed her lips together and picked up her beaded purse.

She was ready.

By the time she walked into the door of the hall, her hands and feet were ice cold and she was shivering inside. She stepped into the hall and was overcome.

The first thing she was noticed was the hum of hundreds of voices underlaid with a soundtrack of classical music playing quietly.

So this is what sold-out looks like, she thought.

People were everywhere; sitting at tables, chatting in corners and bent over the tables lining the edges of an arena that had been miraculously transformed.

Rows and rows of round paper lanterns were strung along the ceiling, each lit up inside. The tables were covered in white linen and yellow runners, and each table held a tall crystal vase holding an assortment of Asiatic lilies, with ivy climbing down the vase to rest on the table.

Dark velvet curtains were draped along the front of the auditorium, creating a backdrop for the stage, which was edged with white linen and draped with ivy, as well.

Her eyes swept the arena, looking for only one person. But she could see no sign of him. He would be here. Of that she was positive.

And that had been why she had hesitated so long. But if she was going to try to live her life here in Riverbend, if she was going to carry on, then she needed to do just that. Carry on. Be herself.

"Dodie. There's the birthday girl."

Dodie put on a smile and turned to face her mother.

"Happy birthday, dear. Tilly pressed a kiss to Dodie's cheek. "My goodness, you're chilled. Your father and I have been looking everywhere for you." Her mother looked elegant in a dark blue velvet dress and silver bolero. Diamonds sparkled from her ears and necklace. Her eyes flicked over Dodie's dress and she frowned. "Didn't you wear that dress to Ethan and Hannah's wedding?"

"Seemed a shame not to use it again."

"Well, it looks lovely enough." Her mother smoothed a strand of hair away from Dodie's face. "I made sure that we're sitting at the same table. All the organizers of the fundraiser will be sitting near the front."

"That's fine, Mom," Dodie said weakly. She was holding herself together by sheer willpower. She hoped that she wouldn't be in Jace's line of vision because that would make it too difficult for her to maintain her composure.

"All the seats are assigned, my dear, and this is a sold-out crowd." Tilly tugged on Dodie's arm as she worked her way through the crowd to the front of the arena.

"Here's our table," Tilly announced. "Dan, look who I found."

Dodie's father was already getting up, smiling at his daughter. He wore a silver-gray suit and black shirt and tie, which only enhanced the few grey strands in his blonde hair. "Lookin' pretty spiff, Dad," Dodie said, giving him a quick hug.

"Happy birthday, my dear, and may you be blessed with many more." Her father returned the hug and pulled back, a concerned look on his face. "I stopped by the coffee shop this week, but Janie said you were sick."

"Yeah. I had some kind of weird bug that just wouldn't go away, but I feel better now."

The squeal of a microphone caught her attention and then the chairman, Randy Webber, was standing at the podium. "Everyone please find your seats," he said pleasantly. "We need to get started."

People made their way back to their tables, and in a matter of minutes everyone was sitting down.

"Let me do that for you, hon," her father said, helping her into her seat.

"Thanks, Dad," Dodie murmured as she sat down. Her gaze skittered over the room, looking for Jace.

But she hadn't seen him.

There was an empty seat beside Dodie and, curious as to who it might be, Dodie glanced at the place card.

And panic uncoiled through her.

Jace Scholte.

Please Lord, help me get through this, she prayed, then assured herself that everything would be just fine.

"I just want to say a hearty welcome to everyone here tonight," Randy said, glancing over the crowd. "We've got a wonderful program for you, and I want to add my congratulations and thanks to Dodie Westerveld and Jace Scholte for getting Helen Lennox to sing for us this evening."

He turned to Dodie and started clapping, and a burst of applause followed.

Dodie felt a flush of pleasure at the acknowledgment, but that was mixed with nervous apprehension. Jace still hadn't shown up and she knew he was going to.

Her mother turned in her seat, surveying the full arena, then turned the other way.

"What's wrong, Tilly?" Dan asked.

"I can't understand where Jace would be. He said he was going to be sitting with us."

Dodie wondered if he had decided to forgo the evening. She felt the faintest flicker of hope. If he didn't come and he had to leave right after the fundraiser, maybe she wouldn't see him at all.

But the sense of loss she felt extinguished the hope. She closed her eyes, struggling to find her equilibrium. Ever since Jace had come back to Riverbend, she felt as if the hold she had on her life had been slowly slipping out of her fingers.

"Sorry I'm late." The sound of a deep, familiar voice shot Dodie's heart into overdrive, and she looked up in time to see Jace settle into the chair beside her.

She swallowed down the beat of anticipation his presence evoked. He wore a black suit, white shirt and gray tie—elegant and appealing.

The intricate ebb and flow of her emotions was exhausting, and when he turned to look at her, she didn't know what to cling to anymore.

"How are you?" he asked, his voice quiet.

She breathed a sigh of relief at his even tone. He was going to play it this way, then. Thank goodness. Anger would have made her angry in return, and sympathy would have worn down her own fragile defenses. Bland and unemotional was exactly the kind of tone she could emulate.

"I'm fine," she said, with a polite nod.

"Happy birthday, by the way." She forced a smile, acknowledging his greeting.

Then Randy was dictating the order the tables would be eating. Theirs was the second one.

Having food in front of her gave her something to concentrate on. Thankfully, her parents and the other people at the table kept the conversation going. Dodie only contributed when spoken to, skating her fork across her plate in a vague attempt at eating.

It was going to be a long evening. She wanted to duck out, to run away, but she fought the urge. She had spent enough of her life running away. She wasn't going to do that anymore.

"And I understand Helen is going to be singing a little longer this evening," her mother said to Jace. "To fill in for the speaker who cancelled."

Jace nodded, and wiped his mouth with a napkin, then laid it on his plate. "We've been pretty blessed that she was able to do this. But it was thanks to Dodie's connections that we were able to get her at all." He shot her a sidelong glance, and for a moment she couldn't look away, pleased at his acknowledgment of her involvement.

"I didn't know that," Tilly responded, her incredulous tone almost, but not quite, wounding Dodie.

Because it was balanced out by Jace's approbation of her.

She looked away though. Nothing had changed. What he had given her was a kind of parting gift. He was still leaving.

Her heart contracted at the thought.

For a few wonderful moments she had envisioned them together. Side by side. But the dream was over and reality had taken its place.

Jace's dreams of working with Carson MacGregor left no room for her. Or for Riverbend.

The conversation drifted along, covering local politics, a new business starting in Riverbend and a myriad of other topics that Dodie had a hard time concentrating on. She was far too aware of Jace sitting so close, yet so far out of reach.

The dinner was followed by a PowerPoint presentation

talking about the center. As soon as it was done and the lights came up, Dodie got up.

"I'd better see how Helen is doing," she said, grateful for the excuse to leave.

Dodie walked to the front of the arena and ducked behind the curtains. Backstage, Helen stood to one side, adorned in a simple off-white dress spangled with sequins, a silky orange shawl draped over her shoulders. She wore her hair loose.

Her hands were twined around each other.

"How are you doing?" Dodie asked.

Helen blew out a sigh. "I'm okay. I guess."

Dodie frowned, noticing Helen's wan look.

"Just a bit of preperformance jitters," Paul said, standing beside her, rubbing his wife's back.

Dodie had had to look twice at Paul. The leather blazer over the open-necked shirt and new blue jeans was surprise enough. But his shining cheeks and neatly groomed hair gave him a dapper air that made Dodie realize what Helen had seen in the man in the first place.

"You're going to do great," Dodie said soothingly, trying to ease Helen's nerves.

A bank of curtains put up for this occasion, hid Helen from the audience. Beyond the curtains Dodie heard Randy. He had moved onto the next part of the program and was giving more information about the center and how the funds from tonight would be used.

"You sure you're going to be okay?" Paul whispered to Helen, looking a bit nervous himself. Helen nodded, but Dodie saw the concern in his eyes as he hovered close to his wife.

"I'll be okay. Just give me a few minutes," Helen said, smoothing her palms down the sides of her dress.

"Okay. There's my cue. I'll go warm up the crowd a bit. I'm leaving her in your capable hands." Paul patted Dodie on the shoulder.

Paul gave Helen a quick kiss, caught his guitar by the neck and disappeared through the curtains onto the stage.

The lights dimmed and soon his mellow voice filled the auditorium.

Helen drew in a long, slow breath as she shook her head, her golden hair spilling down her back. She gave Dodie a pensive smile. "You know this is the first time I've performed since…" Her voice faded off.

As their eyes held, Dodie felt a sudden jolt of awareness. She recalled how Helen had hinted that she had struggled with feelings of inadequacy and self-worth before she met Paul.

"Since what?" she coaxed gently, hoping Helen would confide in her.

Helen paused, as if gathering her thoughts. "That night when you came over…" Her voice drifted off again as she looked back at the stage. "I had a feeling, just a vague idea, that you knew what I've had to deal with."

Dodie thought of the songs she had been listening to the evening of her and Jace's fight. She thought of the connection she felt with the words of loss and pain Helen had sung.

"What do you mean?"

Helen held her gaze as if in challenge. She drew in another breath, as if readying herself. "I mean that my life was torn apart by a man who assaulted me. A man who raped me."

Dodie reached behind her to steady herself as her world spun around. She turned away from Helen's steady gaze. "I…I don't know what you're saying."

Helen's voice softened with pity. "You haven't told anyone, have you?"

Dodie wavered on the edge of confession, but old habits were hard to break.

"Tell them what?"

Helen sighed, then touched Dodie lightly on the shoulder. "You don't need to carry this alone, you know. God is always there to help you carry your griefs, your sorrows, your loss. But so is your family. Your friends."

Dodie swallowed down a knot of pain and sorrow. She glanced through the curtain at Paul, then at Helen.

"You have someone," Dodie said quietly. "Someone who understands you, who feels the same way you do. Someone who shares your values and dreams."

Helen tilted her head then touched Dodie gently on the cheek. "You do, too. I know Jace cares deeply for you."

"Jace cares more for his job. He has his own dreams. After tonight, he's gone," Dodie said.

"Then maybe you should give him a reason to stay."

"And what reason would that be?"

"That you care for him. And I think he needs to know what you've had to deal with," Helen urged.

Dodie thought of the burden she carried and wondered if she ever could put it on Jace's shoulders. Wondered if he would understand. If he would even believe her if she told him who the perpetrator was.

Dodie glanced over her shoulder to the opening in the curtains leading to the stage. She saw Paul, sitting on a stool, still singing and just beyond him, his face lit by the soft glow of the candles on their table, she saw Jace. He was looking in her direction and for a moment she felt a connection.

Could she tell him?

Dodie turned away, the doubts and fears that she had carefully hidden away all these years, awash in her mind.

"We hide because we're ashamed," Helen said, her words striking a chord. "Even though it's not our fault, we still hide, and we hurt and we don't tell anyone. I think if I was more honest, more open, I would have gotten help sooner." Helen laid a light hand on Dodie's shoulder. "People want to help and they want to understand. Like I said, you don't have to carry this burden alone."

Dodie faced her, a faint spark of hope igniting in her. "I'm scared," she whispered.

"Of course you are. So was I. But you have family and community." She paused. "And now, I have a set to perform—and you should get back to that very handsome man who, I think, cares for you more than you realize."

Dodie stood rooted in place, wishing fervently that she could share Helen's confidence about a future with Jace.

Dodie wished she was more confident about that.

Paul finished up the song and was greeted with a warm burst of applause, then Randy came to the microphone again. He thanked Paul and told a couple of jokes that received polite laughter.

Paul came backstage and glanced from Helen to Dodie, concern furrowing his brow.

"Everything okay here?" he asked.

"I'm fine," Helen reassured him. She gave Dodie a knowing smile, then turned to Paul, adjusted the collar of his shirt and patted him lightly on the chest. "Let's go," she said. Then she turned and swept onto the stage, leaving Dodie behind.

Dodie watched as the lights caught the sparkles of Helen's dress, bathing her in an aura of light.

She waited a moment, trying to still the erratic beating

of her heart, then she returned to her table, ignoring a puzzled look from Jace.

She sat back, letting Helen's rich contralto flow over her. Her first few songs were older ones, and she invited people to sing along. She paused between songs to explain how they had come to be, what inspired her to write them and what they meant to her.

As Helen sang and talked, Dodie felt some of the tension gripping her the past week ease away with the folksy, familiar songs and Helen's easy way with the crowd. One would never have guessed that only a few moments ago she was as nervous and uptight as Dodie was now, sitting beside Jace.

She just had to get through this night, Dodie thought, unable to completely block out Jace's profile in her peripheral vision.

In spite of Helen's assurances, the reality was that once this evening was done, he would be gone and out of her life. Working for Carson MacGregor.

Her throat closed off at the thought and for a frightening moment, she felt tears threaten. She swallowed, struggling to stay on top of her emotions. She couldn't break now.

But, in spite of herself, she stole a quick sideways glance his way and her heart pounded when she caught him looking at her.

Their eyes clung and it seemed he was looking for something she didn't dare give him.

The truth.

His gaze softened for a moment and she felt her breath catch in her throat as he raised his hand from the table, as if to touch her.

Then Helen was speaking again and she wrenched her gaze back to the stage.

"This next song comes from a place that I had avoided for many years in my life," Helen was saying, settling onto the stool placed there for her benefit.

She glanced at the lighting director and gave a quick nod.

The arena lights were lowered and Helen, lit by the single spotlight, shone like a beacon.

"I wrote this song out of pain and shame, never thinking I would perform it in public. But tonight, I know I have to." Helen looked at Paul, who smiled back at her, as if encouraging her.

And then, she looked directly at Dodie, as if challenging her.

"When I signed my first recording contract, I thought my life was finally heading down the path I had envisioned for myself since my father bought me my first guitar. My parents had dreams and plans. And so did I. And for many years my dreams were coming true. I had success and adulation. I had money." She looked over the audience again, in that disconcerting way of hers that seemed to see past the facade to hidden secrets. "But I didn't know how badly things would go for me. I didn't know how easily dreams could be shattered, torn and discarded by the actions of one person."

Dodie couldn't stop the quick intake of her breath. She was going to do it, she thought. She was going to bare her soul in front of these complete strangers.

Helen's voice grew lower, more intimate as she related the horrific turn her life took when a man she had put her trust in, a man who had promised to take care of her, had found her alone one night.

As she shared her story, Dodie felt as if Helen was slowly, painstakingly drawing out her own secrets, for all to see.

She felt once again the shame of that evening. The pain. The humiliation. And then the fear.

She wanted Helen to stop, willed the story to end. She couldn't do this.

She had to get out. She had to leave. It was as if the huge arena was pressing in on her, growing smaller, suffocating her.

She pressed her hand to her chest, fighting for breath. *Keep me safe, O God, for in You I take refuge.*

The Bible verse slipped into her mind and she clung to the comfort. She had taken refuge in God. It had taken time. And she would trust that He would help her through this.

And then, to her utter surprise, she felt Jace's hand resting on hers. She gave in to an impulse and curled her fingers around his.

Just these few moments, she thought, relishing the warmth of his touch, savoring the strength of his hand. Just these few more precious moments.

Helen finished the song, but Paul kept lightly strumming his guitar, laying down a gentle counterpoint to her spoken words.

Helen looked around the audience, a smile playing around the edges of her lips. "After I wrote that song, I realized that the journey I was taking was one from thinking myself worthless and unworthy of success and happiness, to God showing me that my value wasn't and isn't in who I am to the world, but who I am to Him."

She pressed her hand to her heart and turned back to Paul. "And, more important, God opened my eyes to a support network I could turn to. I only wish it hadn't taken me so long to find a community to call my own. If I had, it could have made a difference in my recovery."

She faced the audience again.

"I want to challenge all of you to seek out the wounded and weary and give them rest. I received help and hope the moment I let other people into my life and into my pain. I hope this center will give other lost and hurting souls of this community an opportunity to find peace and to accept help."

She paused a moment and then began speaking again.

"So in light of that, I want to sing this last song that I also wrote while living here in Riverbend. A song that is a waypoint for the journey I'm on. I hope this song might give any of you who are struggling with secret sorrow, who are struggling with shame, some hope, some scrap of dignity and courage to face your fears."

She began singing and Dodie felt her heart rejoice with the words. Helen's song was an anthem of hope, of being strong by being weak enough to show hidden pain.

And as she sang, Dodie felt herself receive courage and hope. And with Jace's hand holding hers, she felt strength.

The last note of Helen's clear voice hovered in the hushed auditorium then faded away. A heavy pause, more eloquent than any applause fell on the gathering.

And then people surged to their feet, applauding wildly.

And as Dodie got to her feet, she knew what she had to do.

Jace's hand tightened on hers. "Are you okay?" He leaned closer, speaking just loud enough for her to hear.

She turned to him and reached up and touched her cheek, wiping away a tear she hadn't even realized she had shed.

"What's wrong, Dodie?" The concern in his voice underlined her decision. She hadn't been fair to him and she couldn't let him leave before she bared her soul. She had kept this from him far too long.

She was tired of hiding. Tired of running. As Helen had

said, her value was in how God saw her, not what had happened to her.

And if Jace couldn't handle it, that was his problem, not hers.

She turned to him. "We need to talk."

"Where?"

People were still on their feet, applauding and calling for an encore. Dodie and Jace would not be noticed if they left now.

She walked ahead of him, leading the way. She went backstage, then turned and found an exit. She wanted to be away from people, out in the open, when she finally told him everything.

Chapter Thirteen

The outside air was a welcome chill on Jace's heated cheeks. The tension that had held him in a tight grip had eased as Helen performed.

Helen had been amazing and for that he was doubly thankful. But something in Helen's words had obviously touched Dodie.

Now he was feeling tense again as he followed Dodie away from the arena, toward the small play-park beyond the parking lot. Her hair glimmered in the gathering dusk, and her pale green gown seemed to shine with its own ethereal light.

When he had seen her sitting at the table, she had taken his breath away. He'd had to fight the urge to catch her by the hand, pull her away from the crowd and demand answers.

And that worked so well for you the last time, he thought with a touch of cynicism.

The streetlights were just flickering on as dusk settled into the sky. A faint breeze whispered through the large trees overhead as Dodie walked toward a small picnic table beside a large slide.

She paused a moment, her hand toying with the beads at her neckline, then she sat down.

Jace wanted to maintain the advantage by standing. "You said we have to talk," he said, towering above her. "Why don't you start?"

Dodie folded her hands on her lap, not looking at him, her gaze focused on something just beyond him. She didn't say anything right away but Jace knew that sooner or later she would fill the silence.

"Remember that summer I left?" she said, her voice soft. Composed.

"When you took off without a word? Yes." How did she think he could possibly have forgotten?

"Something happened to me—"

"In Europe?"

"No. Before that." She drew a long, slow breath, her shoulders rising and falling. "The night before I left, I was working late. At the office." She stopped there, looking down at her hands, now twisted together on her lap. "I was doing some photocopying for the case you and Chuck and I were supposed to be working on. The machine had jammed and I was bent over it, checking something out. Carson came up behind me. Made some comment about me teasing him. I thought he was joking. Then he grabbed me and spun me around."

Jace frowned even as a chill crept through his veins.

She started talking faster, her words spilling out, falling over themselves as she described what happened next.

Jace felt his blood run cold as she spoke.

"And when he was done, he told me I asked for it, had been asking for it since I started working for him. Told me it was my fault. Told me not to tell anyone and if I did, he would deny it. He said no one would believe me if I said anything and that if I did, he would lay libel charges against me." A tremor filled her voice. "I was afraid of him. I'd read his case files. I knew how tough and how powerful and persistent he could be. I saw him eviscerate witnesses on the stand. I was terrified and I was desperately ashamed. I didn't dare tell my parents. Or you. I didn't dare tell you."

The cold became splinters of ice that stabbed him with each of her words.

"He raped you?" His words came out on a whisper, as if saying them any louder would give them too much substance.

Dodie nodded, then looked up at him. Her features were an expressionless mask, as if she didn't dare show any emotion.

"Carson MacGregor…?" Jace just stared down at her beautiful face—her innocent face—as he tried to imagine the man he had admired for so long, the man he owed so much to, doing this unspeakable thing.

He couldn't think. He didn't know what to process first.

His girlfriend, the woman he had once thought of as pure…an innocent.

Raped by his boss?

Jace couldn't wrap his head around the idea.

"You're the first one I told this to," Dodie said, her voice quiet in the evening air. "Not even my parents know."

Jace closed his eyes, trying to focus. Trying to figure out where to put this new information.

Please, Lord, I don't know what to do with this, he prayed. *I don't know how to comprehend this.*

He walked away, to give himself some space, some

room to think, to understand the implications of this horrible admission. He leaned back against the kiddie slide, the hard metal of the posts digging into his back.

Last week he had thought he and Dodie would be able to put the past behind them. And for a few precious moments tonight he held on to a tenuous hope that she might change her mind. Might be willing to move with him to Edmonton.

But this? Could they really get past this?

She had told him for a reason. And now that she had told him, so many more things fell in place. Dodie's sudden departure that summer. How she had cut him out of her life. The complete change she had made in her behavior when she came back. It all made sense now.

What shame she must have felt.

He was about to turn back to her, to give her what comfort he could when a voice called out.

"Dodie, there you are. I've been looking all over for you."

Jace came around the slide in time to see Dodie's mother drop onto the bench beside her.

"Goodness, girl, your arms are like ice. What are you doing out here all alone without a wrap?" Tilly put her arm around Dodie and gave her a hug. "You've got to come back to the arena. We've got a special surprise for you."

Dodie wasn't even looking at her mother. Her eyes were focused on him. And all he could do was stare back at her.

"Come now, don't dilly-dally," Tilly was saying, pulling Dodie to her feet. "People are waiting."

As Tilly led Dodie out of the park, she suddenly saw Jace. "My goodness…" Her voice faltered as she glanced from Dodie to Jace, then back to her daughter. "I'm sorry, I didn't think I was interrupting anything—"

"You weren't, Mother," Dodie said, her voice flat. "Jace was just leaving." She glanced over at Jace, gave him a tight nod, then left with her mother, taking his chance with him.

Jace watched them go, his heart sinking with every footstep she took away from him.

He had messed up. He should not have turned away from her. But what else could he have done? This had completely blindsided him.

Carson MacGregor raped my girlfriend.

Those words were an abomination to him. The two most important people in his life and…this?

Jace shoved his hands through his hair and grabbed the back of his neck. He had to get out of here. He had to think. To decide what he was going to do.

He started walking. He didn't have any plan in mind, he just needed to keep moving.

Was Dodie right about Carson?

He felt the clutch of disloyalty. How could he think she was lying?

And yet…Carson? The man he had looked up to? The man he owed his career to?

Please, Lord, I need Your guidance, he prayed once again. *I don't know where to go from here.*

Strains of "Happy Birthday" followed him as he walked away from the noisy arena, toward the quiet of the town. The bottom of his world had fallen out and he had no ground on which to stand. No firm place that he could find his balance.

So he kept wandering aimlessly through the town he grew up in. His feet led him down Main Street, through one puddle of light after another, his steps echoing on the quiet street in time to the words he could not erase from his mind.

Carson raped Dodie.

He strolled past darkened stores, past Janie's coffee shop, past his own office. He turned the corner and headed down the street that led downhill, down toward the river. As he moved along, he reached for his phone a dozen times, only to pull his hand back.

He shouldn't have walked away from Dodie.

He paused briefly when he came to the park he and Dodie had their picnic and from there, continued up the street again until he came to Dodie's apartment. The lights were off.

His mind raced back to the fight they'd had. How he'd come demanding answers and she'd ordered him out.

He followed the street, then turned again until he came to his house. He stood there a moment as memories slipped back into his mind. Memories of how eager he was to leave this place.

Yet, since coming back, he'd seen a different perspective on his parent's lives here. Yes, they hadn't had much money, and yes, things had been difficult, but his memories didn't jibe with other people's perspectives of his family.

Could I stay here? he thought.

He thought of Dodie and his stomach clenched again. Would she take me? he asked himself.

He shoved his hands in the pockets of his suit jacket. His one hand hit something and he drew out the long, narrow box. Dodie's birthday present. He had forgotten to give it to her.

He had bought it at the farmer's market, the day before he and Dodie had gone to pick up the chair from Mr. DeVries. The day he and Dodie had decided to try again. Start over.

Now what?

He couldn't think that far. He knew he had messed up with Dodie, but he had no way to prepare for what she had told him.

Please, Lord, give her strength, give her comfort, he prayed as he walked into his house. As he fell into bed, he prayed for strength for what he had to do tomorrow.

"Surely you don't believe I would do something like that?" Carson MacGregor leaned back in his leather chair, one corner of his mouth curved up in a cynical smile. The overhead light glinted off his graying hair, styled to perfection, giving him the patrician air that served him so well in court. His suit rested perfectly on his broad shoulders, the silk tie cinching his blinding white shirt, giving off the sheen of money.

Confronting Carson in his office had been a tactical error, but Jace didn't want to go to Carson's home. Thankfully Carson was a workaholic, so Jace had got up early Sunday morning and driven straight to the city, knowing he would find his boss in his office hard at work. And while Jace made the two-hour drive from Riverbend to the city, he prayed for Dodie and the pain she had endured all these years.

But mostly, he prayed for wisdom and strength to do what he knew needed to be done.

He prayed as he parked in the parking lot, as he walked up every single flight of stairs to Carson's twentieth-floor office suite.

Carson had been in his office, as Jace had suspected. He had come right to the point.

"These are pretty strong accusations to make, my boy," Carson said, his voice growing silky and quiet, the way he did in court before he would suddenly twist and skewer a witness on his own inconsistencies.

"I phrased it as a question, Carson." Jace kept his own voice even as he shifted his weight on the wooden chair. "I need to know if what she says is true."

Carson emitted a short laugh that held a note of disdain. "Dodie Westerveld has proven to be a flighty, irresponsible young girl. She left us in the lurch during a very important court case with no explanation whatsoever." He slowly got up, his movements deliberate as he walked around his desk. He stopped in front of Jace and rested one hip on the desk, looking down with a patronizing expression. "I highly doubt the testimony of a slightly disturbed woman could be taken very seriously. And I think you would be wise to realize this."

Jace tried to sort his emotions, to pull back from what Carson was saying and focus on what he wasn't saying.

"You still haven't answered my question."

Carson's jaw clenched. "Are you cross-examining me in my own office?"

Jace wanted to stand, to put himself on equal footing with his boss. Having the man looking down on him was disquieting, and he realized how Carson could easily intimidate a witness.

"I'm merely asking a question. Is what Dodie told me true?" His heart was hammering in his chest.

Carson rose to his full height, making a slight adjustment to the front of his coat. He shook his head, a slow movement that didn't bode well for Jace.

"There's no room in this law firm for someone who presumes to question my integrity, so I'm going to make this very clear. Either you drop this heinous lie that Miss Westerveld is trying to foist upon you, or you leave."

Carson raised his palm toward the door behind Jace. "Simple as that."

Jace felt himself on shaky ground again as he reflected all the years and time and money he had put into getting to where he was. For so long, his dream had been to work for Carson MacGregor. Now, it hung in the balance.

He knew his job was at risk when he came here. And he also knew that a lawyer of Carson's stature would never have admitted to anything criminal just because he was confronted with it.

But Jace needed to see him face-to-face. To hear the man that he'd respected for so long, looked up to so long, say that Dodie was wrong. But he hadn't said anything one way or the other.

Which was enough for Jace.

Jace took a long, slow breath as he got to his feet. "My choice is clear. I'm sorry, Carson. I can't work with you."

Carson stared at him, as if he couldn't believe what Jace was saying, then his mouth tightened, his eyes narrowed and he drew back. "You'd better think this through very carefully, Jace. If you walk out that door, it's over. I won't ask you back."

"If I walk through that door, I won't come back."

Carson's expression grew thunderous. "You're throwing your whole career away for the sake of this…woman."

For a moment Jace stared at his former boss, then let his eyes tick around the room, looking over the certificates, the degrees, the accolades that Carson had amassed in his life. Once Jace had wanted all this for himself. The corner office with the amazing view of the river valley in all its spring glory. The huge desk, the high-profile clients. The respect and the money,

Then his gaze returned to Carson, the man he had once idealized, the man he would have done so much for and had. In that moment, he realized that he was wrong to put so much on one human being.

Then, even as the respect he'd once had for this man receded, it was replaced with an anger so all-consuming that he had to step away.

This man had almost destroyed the woman he loved. Almost.

Thankfully, Dodie was stronger than that.

"And I would suggest you stay away from Riverbend for a while, because if I see you I won't be responsible for my actions," Jace ground out, his hands curled into tight fists.

His anger roiled in his gut, and without another word to Carson he spun around and strode out of his office, not even bothering to close the door behind him.

"Don't walk away from me, Jace," he heard Carson calling out, as he strode past the empty desks of the other lawyers' secretaries. The competition. The ones who had also been vying for the position he'd hoped would someday be his.

They can have it, he thought, walking past his own office without a second glance.

"You'll regret this," Carson yelled, as Jace pushed the button for the elevator. Changing his mind, Jace headed to the stairs and charged down them, venting his anger with each step he took.

He didn't know how he got back to Riverbend. The drive was a blur. He pulled up to his house and when he took his clenched hands off the steering wheel of the car, they were trembling.

You've thrown it all away.

For a moment he felt a throb in his gut. He drew in a breath and another, calming himself.

No. Carson threw it all away. And Jace had been a fool to have done his bidding for so many years.

Jace slammed his hand against the steering wheel. Dodie had been hurt, damaged…violated by the man Jace had wanted to emulate.

And how was he supposed to face her now? What could he possibly say to her after he left her alone? After he ran out on her?

She had run away from him once before. Maybe she'd been right to do that. Maybe he couldn't handle what she had to tell him.

Jace put the car back into gear and drove back to Dodie's apartment. He put his car in Park, then waited, gathering his courage.

Please, Lord, give me the right words, he prayed, looking up at her apartment. *Give me the strength to be a support to her. To do the right thing.* He stopped, wishing he knew what to do.

All his lawyer training was no help at this moment. He simply had to rely on the feelings he had for Dodie and hope, by some small miracle, she still felt something for him.

And if not, then he would simply have to either be patient, or learn to live without her.

That last thought choked him. Even during the six years she had kept her distance, some small part of him lived in hope.

"Thy will be done," Jace prayed as he got out of the car. "I just want what's best for Dodie."

He pulled open the door and walked up the stairs, his heart thumping in his chest.

He stopped in front of her door, took a deep breath and lifted his hand to knock.

The door opened and Dodie stood in the doorway.

She looked up and jumped.

"Sorry," he said. "I was just going to knock."

She just stared at him, her hair loose, curled at the ends. She wore a navy cardigan over a white shirt tucked into neatly pressed blue jeans.

Conservative, put together.

Dodie.

She lifted a trembling hand to her chest. "What do you want?"

Jace stared at her, taking in her eyes, her soft vulnerable mouth.

"Can I come in?"

"Um. I was just on my way to see my parents."

"This won't take long."

Dodie stepped back and he followed her into her apartment, closing the door behind them. They went directly to the living room, the place of their last confrontation.

He couldn't help but recall her angry words, telling him to leave. He understood so much better now where they had come from.

"Did you want something to drink? Some tea? Coffee?" she asked, laying her purse on the coffee table.

"No. I just need…to talk a minute."

She lowered herself to her couch and Jace sat down across from her. He leaned forward, his elbows on his knees, his eyes on her.

How much had changed in the past twenty-four hours. Last night he was employed, moving up the corporate ladder, and confused about the woman who now sat across from him.

Now he was unemployed, but knew so much more about Dodie.

"I came to say I'm sorry." He clasped his hands, meeting her gaze. "I'm sorry that I reacted the way I did last night."

Dodie leaned back, folding her arms over her midriff. "I'm guessing you had no clue what I was going to say."

"It blindsided me." Jace hesitated, struggling to find his footing in this new place. He wanted to be sitting beside her. Touching her. Creating a connection between them....

But he had forfeited that right when he walked out on her last night. So he stayed where he was.

"I want to say that I'm sorry for taking off on you when I should have been here. At your side. Helping you. Supporting you. Trying to understand what happened."

"My mom's timing wasn't the best," Dodie admitted. "She didn't want the birthday cake to go stale."

Her comment and the tiny lift of one corner of her mouth gave him a tiny flicker of hope.

"What you told me," he continued, "I didn't know where to put it. What to do with it. I couldn't imagine what it was like for you." He wished his words didn't come out in such a rush, but he felt as if he had only a limited time to plead his case. "You meant so much to me. I had such high hopes for us. When you left, it was like my world fell apart, but had I known what happened to you, I would have followed you, found you, tried to help you through it all."

She held his gaze and he could see pain in her eyes. Pain that he longed to erase.

"For six years I wondered why you left," he said, pitching his voice low as he tried to stay in control of his emotions. "I had speculated on all kinds of scenarios.

Went over everything I had ever said or done to you. I talked to all your friends. I phoned your parents, bugged your sister. You know how I tried to contact you. I almost broke into your apartment to see if I could find out anything from there."

Her gaze shifted to her hands, folded in front of her, but he sensed she was listening.

"I knew nothing, but I speculated about everything. When I was back in town the last time you avoided me, so I figured it was something I did but couldn't remember. And then, I'm back again and I think, 'Okay, I'll eventually find out exactly what happened.' So last night when you finally told me everything, it was so far from anything I had imagined during that six-year separation. I just didn't know where to put it."

"And you didn't think Carson was capable of something like that." She looked up at him, as if daring him to deny what she said.

He couldn't evade her direct statement, couldn't hide behind any excuse.

"No. I couldn't. That's what made me so confused."

She looked away and Jace felt a surge of frustration. He ignored caution and sat beside her. He turned her to face him. "You had just pulled out the foundations of a life I had been building for six years based on an admiration of a man I'd known far longer. A man who helped pay for my education, a man who had given me an opportunity that no one else had. He was like my own father." He let out a long, shuddering breath. "And then I find out this man, this mentor, had done this unspeakable thing to you—the woman I have always loved and always cared for. The woman who meant everything to me."

Dodie closed her eyes, as if unable to look at him anymore, but he persevered.

"It wasn't a matter of choosing you over Carson, Dodie, it was a matter of me trying to figure out how to put back together the pieces of my life that had been ripped apart." He loosened his grip, but stroked her arms with his hands, trying to make her understand, praying she would understand. "I love you so much, Dodie. And to think that this happened to you and I wasn't able to help you—" He stopped, his emotions choking off coherent thought.

"I thought you didn't believe me," she whispered, her head still bent.

Jace took a chance and gently tilted her head up. He held her wounded gaze, then slowly lowered his mouth and kissed her. He drew back and cupped her face in his hands, stroking her cheeks with his thumb.

"I love you and, if it wasn't illegal, I would do some serious damage to Carson MacGregor, something far more serious than quitting my job."

Dodie's shining eyes told him more than any words she could have spoken. And when she pulled his head down to kiss him back, his heart sang with relief and with love.

"I thought you couldn't stand to be with me," she said, her voice ragged. "I thought you were disgusted because I wasn't the same innocent, untouched girl I once was."

"No, Dodie. Never." Jace's heart broke at the anguish in her voice. He didn't like seeing the strong, vivacious girl he had come to respect come to this. "You're still Dodie. You're still a child of God and you're still loved by Him. And by me."

Dodie's laugh held a note of irony. "You love me. Now."

He gently smoothed a tendril of hair back from her

face. "I think I always have. I just needed to find a way to express it."

Dodie shook her head, as if unable to comprehend what he was telling her. "You love me," she said again, testing the words.

"I love you. And I admire you. You dealt with this on your own, you stayed strong. You carried on and created your own life—"

"Hardly a life."

Jace gave her a gentle shake. "When I see what you have done for so many members of this community, I realize that you *did* do the things that we had in mind when we first wanted to be lawyers. You are serving and interacting with people in so many beneficial ways. Ways that I know are probably more pleasing to God than many of the things I've done with my expensive education and golden opportunities."

Dodie swiped a stray tear off her cheek. "You're just trying to make me feel good."

"Do you?"

She blinked, then slowly turned her head to him, a smile feathering her lips. "A bit."

Jace cradled her shoulders with his hands. "You've become the person I wanted to be. Someone who helps other people without thinking about yourself. And in spite of what happened to you—or maybe because of it—I see you as more determined to make your own way. To do what you want and not what other people expect."

He drew her close, wrapping his arms around her. He was too late to protect her from what had happened, but as much as it was in his power, he was going to keep her safe. Keep her close.

She laid her head against his shoulder, returned his

embrace as she nestled against him. "I didn't think this would ever happen," she murmured. "I didn't think I would be able to be with you, after you knew."

Jace held her even tighter, as if to let her know how wrong she was.

He felt her draw in a trembling breath. And then another as she sniffed.

"It's okay, Dodie. I'm here," he said quietly, sensing what was coming. "I'm not going to leave you. I'm not going to let you go."

The first trembling sob cut into his soul. Then came the next.

And then she was turning to him, her body wracked with sorrow, tears flowing from her eyes onto his shirt. She clung to him, as sobs convulsed her body and leached out the pain and loss of the last six years.

Jace closed his eyes, holding her tightly to him, his head pressed on hers, as his own tears flowed.

Then after a time, the storm slowly subsided and her sobs turned into broken breaths.

"I'm sorry, Dodie. I'm so sorry." Jace rocked her gently back and forth, holding her as close as he dared, wishing he could have protected her.

She lay against him and her hand clutched his shoulder. "I'm sorry I made your shirt wet."

Through his own tears, Jace had to smile. "It will dry."

Then Dodie drew away, her hands pushing at her hair. "I must look a wreck," she sniffed.

Her eyes were red and twin tracks of mascara ran down her cheeks. Her hair was disheveled.

But to Jace she was the most beautiful woman in the world. He got up, retrieved a box of tissues and handed them to her, placing one hand on her shoulder while she tidied up.

The digitized sound of a bird chirping coming from the pocket of Dodie's jacket, broke into the moment.

Jace hoped she would ignore it, but she wiped her eyes once more.

"I'm sorry," she murmured, digging into her pocket. "Probably my mom. I told her I would be right over."

Jace kept his hand on her shoulder, however, anchoring a gentle calm to her.

Dodie sniffed again, then flipped open the phone. "Hey, Mom… Yeah… I'll be right there," she said, giving Jace a tender smile. "Yes, I know I told you it was important but, well…I'm just running a bit late is all." She smiled, nodded and then said goodbye. She took a deep, shaky breath and got up. "I gotta go tidy up. Be right back."

A few minutes later she returned and, except for her still-red eyes, looked freshened up. "Will I pass?"

Jace nodded as he rubbed his thumb over her cheek, wiping away a tiny smudge of mascara. "You were going to your folks' place?"

Dodie nodded pressing her hands to her flushed cheeks. "Now that I've told you, it's time I tell them, too."

"You kept this quiet from everyone?"

"Like I said, I felt so ashamed and I was scared of Carson. And so I kept silent. And then one year became two, then three, and after a while, I thought maybe I could forget about it. And then you returned and we started spending time together…and you were such a reminder to me of everything from before and it all came rushing back."

"I'm sorry, Dodie. I'm so sorry." He gave her a quick hug. "I'll go with you if you want."

"Really?"

Jace grew serious. "I don't want you to do this on your own."

"That would be better than great," she said. "I know they need to be told, but I'm so scared to tell them."

"Of course you are. This is hard."

"I'm a nervous wreck. I've spent the last two hours trying to figure out what to wear, what to say and how to let them know why I've kept this from them for so long."

"You don't need to explain anything, Dodie. Just tell them. I think that will be enough for now." He stroked her face again.

"I'm still worried," she said as she leaned into him.

Jace brushed a kiss over her head and sent up a prayer that her parents would understand.

Chapter Fourteen

"He did what?" Tilly shot up from the couch, her hands clenched into fists.

"When did this happen?" Dodie's father spoke through gritted teeth.

Her parents' shock was like a tidal wave battering her fragile defenses.

Dodie was thankful for Jace's presence beside her, for his arm around her shoulder, supporting and holding her up.

"All this time…" Her mother's voice trembled. "All this time and you never told us."

Dodie felt once again the shame and guilt that had been her constant companion since that horrible night.

"When you went to Europe we thought it was because of stress, because of your work…" Her mother strode across the room, then turned as if seeing Dodie for the first time.

Dan Westerveld looked up at her, his expression twisted with anguish. "Honey, why didn't you tell us?"

Her mother's anger wasn't a surprise, but the brokenness in her father's voice was her undoing.

"I couldn't, Daddy. I was so ashamed. I felt so…dirty." Her voice wavered. She struggled to maintain control. Her head still ached from the gale of tears she had shed in her apartment. A storm that Jace had been there to hold her through.

Dan's narrowed gaze zeroed in on Jace. "Did you know your boss did this?"

"I just found out on Saturday—"

"Dodie, you couldn't tell us? Your own parents?" Tilly's shrill voice cut through the dull, throbbing pain in Dodie's head. She knew this was going to be bad, she just hadn't expected so much anger from her mother. "How could you have held this back from us?" Tilly continued, her voice growing sharper.

"I think, right now, Dodie needs your support more than your anger," Jace said.

Dodie sank against him in relief.

"Don't presume to tell me how I should behave right now," Tilly snapped. "My daughter was hurt in the most shameful, heinous way…only another woman could understand how humiliating this could be. And it was your boss that did it."

Dodie closed her eyes, trying to weather out this storm, thankful for Jace's arm around her, creating a sanctuary of understanding and support. She knew this would be hard, she just didn't think she would feel so emotionally fragile.

"Tilly, please come here and sit down," Dan said. He spoke quietly, but there was a command in his words.

Dodie heard footsteps, then the next thing she knew, she was being drawn to her feet. She opened her eyes and saw her father looking down at her, his own eyes filled with tears, his hands on her shoulder. Her mother stood beside him.

"My baby girl. You carried this all alone, all this time. I'm so sorry." Then she was being held close to her father's chest, surrounded by her father's love. He held her tight, as if trying to give her the protection he hadn't been able to all those years ago. He rocked her gently and to her surprise and amazement, she felt his tears dampening her hair. "I'm so sorry, so sorry."

Her mother was stroking her head, her other hand clinging to Dodie's arm. "My baby girl," she whispered in a broken voice. "My little baby girl."

They stood thus for another moment as Dodie recognized that the hurt she had felt had also been her parents'.

As a father pities his children...

The fragment of the Bible verse eased past her guilt and grief, and she realized that as much as her parents were hurting for her, God hurt, as well.

"Can we pray together?" Tilly said, the sorrow in her voice creating a new wave of sorrow in Dodie's.

Dodie nodded, pulling away from her father, who kept one arm across her shoulders. Tilly had her arm through Dodie's and Jace came to stand opposite her.

She felt surrounded and supported, just as Helen spoke of the night of the fundraiser.

Dodie lowered her head and her father began.

"Lord, You are a father and You know sorrow and pain. You know what we're feeling right now. We don't know what to do for our little girl, or how to help her, but we trust You will show us the way. We want her to feel our love, our caring and our trust. We want her to feel Your love, too. Help us to give her the support and help she needs. Lord, this is more than she should bear, but we know You have given her strength and will. Keep giving her the strength to get through this." He paused a moment and cleared his throat. Then whispered a quiet "Amen."

Dodie kept her eyes closed as a wave of pure, unadulterated love swept over her. She let its purity and strength cleanse her, absolve her.

Then, as she raised her head, Tilly drew her close, giving her a hug. "I'm sorry, honey," she choked out. "I'm so sorry I wasn't a better mother. I'm sorry I didn't recognize what you needed."

"It wasn't your fault, Mom," Dodie said, laying her head on her mother's shoulder. "I should have told you, but I was scared."

"Of course." Tilly stroked her head, then pressed a quick kiss to her forehead. "Of course you were." Then she drew away, standing back to look at her, as if to assess her daughter through this new information.

An awkward moment followed, everyone seemingly unsure of what role they were supposed to play now.

"Would you like a cup of tea or coffee?" Tilly said, her voice taking on a brisk, businesslike tone.

Dodie glanced at Jace. "It's up to you," she said quietly, hoping he would furnish her with some excuse. She needed to leave to get her bearings again.

And she wanted to be with Jace, to rediscover their relationship. There were no more secrets between them, and she was eager to explore this new place they had found. Eager to get to know him with nothing between them.

But to her disappointment, he nodded. "I wouldn't mind juice or a glass of water."

She frowned at him, wondering why he wanted to stay and he gave her an encouraging smile.

"I'll get us all something to drink." Her mother hurried

off to the kitchen, and Dodie knew she was thankful to have a job to do.

Her father sat across from them, his eyes heavy with regret.

"I'm okay, Daddy," she said. "Truly."

Her father wrapped his hands around each other and rocked back and forth a bit. "I want you to know that whatever you want to do, you have our support. Whatever you want to do." His heavy emphasis on that last phrase sent a chill down Dodie's spine. She hadn't thought any further than telling her parents. Confronting Carson...

She couldn't think of that right now and wasn't sure she could.

"I think we'll take this one step at a time, for now," Jace said. "I'll be able to help Dodie if she needs any legal assistance. If she wants to press any charges."

Dodie felt a chill again. She wasn't sure she wanted to think about that yet.

"And what *are* your plans?" Dan asked.

"I've decided to start working on my own," Jace said, assuring her father. "I've quit my job with Carson."

"When?"

"This morning. As soon as I possibly could."

Dan nodded, as if approving.

"I was thinking about some of my options on the way home, and I think I could quite easily start my own legal practice here in Riverbend."

"So you have a plan for your future," Dan said.

Jace nodded, tightening his arm around Dodie's shoulders.

Then Tilly returned with a tray of glasses, ice clinking against the sides. She handed them out, then sat down.

Jace held his glass between his hands, swirling the

juice in a circle. He looked nervous and Dodie wondered what was going on.

He took a sip, then set the glass down. He glanced from her father to her mother, then to Dodie.

"Dan, Tilly, I know this might not be the right time for this, but I also think I've been patient." He cleared his throat and took Dodie's hand in his. "But I'd like to ask for your blessing. I would like to ask Dodie to marry me."

Dodie's heart stopped, did a slow turn, then raced. Jace wanted to propose to her? She squeezed her hand in return, letting him know her own intentions.

Her mother had her hands over her mouth and her father was smiling.

"Well, now, I think that's wonderful," Dan Westerveld said, getting to his feet. He took Jace's hand and laid his other hand on Jace's shoulder. "I am honored to give you our blessing."

Her mother squealed then caught Dodie by the hands, and pulled her up into another fierce hug. "Oh, my baby girl," she said, her voice breaking. "A wedding to plan."

Dodie just smiled and returned her mother's hug.

Tilly pulled back, her eyes shining. "We've got so much to talk about—"

"And so do Dodie and I," Jace said, taking her free hand. "And I'm sorry to rush off."

"No. That's fine," Dan said. "You two go."

Tilly frowned. "But Dodie, we should start making plans—"

"And so should they," Dan put his arm around his wife's shoulders, gently drawing her aside.

Then her father turned to her and gave her another tremulous smile. "You take care of yourself, honey. And please, let us know if you need anything."

"I will. This time." Dodie stood on tiptoe and gave her father a kiss, then her mother, thankful for their love. Their caring and their assurance.

And then she left, her arm tucked into Jace's. She had no idea where they were supposedly going, but for now it didn't matter.

They were together.

They got back into Jace's car and he started driving. The silence was comforting and Dodie felt herself go boneless, felt the tension that had gripped her so tightly, slowly dissipate.

It was done.

"Where are we going?" Dodie asked, finally breaking the silence.

"You'll see." He reached across the car and took her hand in his.

She wanted to ask him a myriad of questions, but she voiced only the one foremost in her mind.

"So you're going to stay in Riverbend?"

Jace nodded. "Regardless of who Carson sends here, Riverbend could use another lawyer's office." Jace gave her a gentle smile. "The money won't be as good—"

"Does that matter?"

"Maybe. But not as much as it used to, and I think it will be good for me to be on my own. Make my own decisions."

Dodie felt herself daring to dream and make a few plans of her own.

Then Jace made a turn off the road, and Dodie knew exactly where they were going. The lookout point.

"And once again, we're trespassing," Dodie said.

"I called Logan this time," Jace told her. "He said it was okay."

"Well, if my cousin's husband says so, then it must be so."

Jace finally came to a stop and turned off the engine. The sudden quiet pressed in on Dodie, but she welcomed it. They got out of the car and Jace reached out a hand to Dodie, then led her to the edge of the bank overlooking the river.

The valley spread away from them, trees newly leafed out and catching the sun. Below them the river sparkled and danced, moving relentlessly onward.

Then Jace turned to her. "I've imagined this moment so many times, practiced so many speeches. Planned all kinds of elaborate scenarios." He smiled at her and cupped her cheek in his hand. Then he put his hand in his pocket and pulled out a small velvet box.

Dodie swallowed, her heart tripping over itself as she looked into Jace's eyes.

"But basically, I have only one thing to ask you." Jace flipped open the box to reveal a diamond ring that flashed in the sun like a promise of bright tomorrows. "Dodie Westerveld, will you marry me?"

Dodie pressed her lips together, as tears threatened once again. But these were happy, joyful tears.

She could only nod and throw her arms around Jace. "Yes. I will."

They stood this way for a moment, warmed by the sun, by their embrace and by their love for each other.

Then Dodie pulled away, and Jace gently fit the simple band with its single diamond on her finger. She held it up, turning it so that it caught the sun and sent it back to her in a myriad of sparkles and colors. "It's beautiful, Jace."

Jace kissed her gently on the lips. "Not as beautiful as the woman wearing it."

She smiled. "Did you make that up?"

He shook his head. "Read it in a magazine."

She laughed aloud and the sound echoed back. "I love you, Jace Scholte. And I want to spend the rest of my life being your devoted wife."

"Did you make that up?" he teased.

"Yes, I did."

He kissed her again. "And I love you…and though I want to spent the rest of my life with you, for now I want to spend some ordinary time with you. Catch up. Find out everything I missed out on. Just be together. Just be Dodie and Jace."

Dodie stoop on tiptoe and brushed a kiss over his one cheek. Then the other. "That will keep us busy for a while. We've got six years to catch up on." She angled him a shy glance, feeling a measure of contentment she hadn't felt since the last time she was with him.

"I know what you gave up for me, Jace," she said, knowing it needed to be said. "I know what Carson meant to you at one time. And I know how disappointed you must be, to have the man you so admired revealed like this."

"I think part of my disappointment is in myself. That I misjudged his character so badly." Jace shook his head. "And even worse, I want to do some serious damage to him." He turned back to Dodie. "And what about you. What do you want to do?"

Dodie knew he was referring to Carson. Pressing charges against him was the last thing on her mind right now.

"How about we save that for another time? I don't want the past to mess up this moment."

Jace shook his head as if in disbelief. "I can't believe you can brush that aside." He gently fingered away a strand of hair caught in her lipstick.

"Hardly brushing. I spent six years suppressing. But now that it's out, I feel strangely free. Something Helen said has helped. Something about the thing that destroys me is the thing that controls me. And you know how much I hate being controlled."

"Except it didn't destroy you."

Dodie sighed and gave him a wistful smile. "No, but it did twist me around. And it made me lose you."

"You never really lost me. Maybe misplaced me for a while." Jace trailed his finger down her neck. "And maybe I needed that time to figure out what I really wanted. Maybe I needed to realize how important you really were to me and how unimportant my job is."

"It's not unimportant," she protested, pressing her hands against his chest. "You can do so much."

"And I can do it here. With the woman I love."

"Will you miss the hustle and bustle of a big-city law firm? Will you feel like you've come back to the place you tried to leave?"

"Being here and being involved with the fundraiser has definitely helped me figure out the benefits of being back in Riverbend. And has made me see this town through adult eyes. Made me realize why my parents stayed here." He lifted her hand and kissed her fingertips. "And made me realize why you came back here."

"To hide."

"And to heal."

Dodie traced the line of his lips. "I'm so thankful that you came back, Jace. God has blessed me beyond blessing."

"Are you still angry with God?"

Dodie puckered her forehead, weighing the question. "When I think of my dad's reaction when I told him about the rape and when I think that God loves me even more than my father, then no. I'm not angry with Him anymore. Because God has set me in this place, in Riverbend, and the boundaries of my life are good. And if you stay, I have all I need. Right here. Close to home."

"I'm glad." Jace caught her hands in his and dropped another kiss on her lips. "And I'm so humbly thankful that you're willing to be with me. I love you so much, Dodie."

She lifted her face to his, her smile brighter than the sun even as tears of joy gathered in her eyes.

"And I love you, Jace."

She sealed her love with a kiss.

And then drifted into the safety of his arms.

Epilogue

"Anything exciting?" Dodie asked, as Jace sauntered into the kitchen and dropped the mail onto the kitchen table.

"Just some bills for the renovation we did on the bathroom." He pulled a face, but then pressed a quick kiss on his wife's forehead. Then he turned her to face him. "You are beautiful."

"Now you're talking like a lawyer. I've got no makeup on, my hair is a disaster and I feel like I've swallowed a whale." Dodie pressed her hands on her stomach, pushing the baby over to one side. "A whale that won't lay still."

"Busy little guy," Jace said, stroking her protruding stomach.

"Or girl."

"Are you sure you don't want to find out what he or she is?" Jace asked, sorting through the envelopes.

"There are precious few pleasant surprises these days, I think I should be allowed at least one." Dodie murmured.

Jace picked up the folded newspaper and went utterly still.

"What's wrong, Jace?" she asked in alarm.

Jace glanced at her, then at her stomach where their child was still moving and twisting.

"Jace, please."

"It's nothing." He snapped the paper shut and tucked it under his arm.

"Come back here," Dodie said, grabbing him. "Let me see."

Jace sighed and then gave in, knowing she would find out eventually. He set the paper down on the table and wordlessly pointed to a small article below the fold. No pictures, just the headline: Lawyer Found Guilty of Sexual Assault."

Dodie let the words register and then grabbed for a chair. Jace caught her and eased her down, supporting her.

"It's done" was all she said.

Jace rubbed her arms, his eyes on her. "Are you okay? Do you want a drink of water? Something?"

She shook her head, dragged her hands over her face and felt the last unspoken burden fall off her shoulders. She had laid her charges and of course Carson denied them. Time had been her enemy and the case had dragged on. Dodie had grown tired and wanted to leave it be.

Then another girl came forward, this time with proof. And justice was finally meted out.

"Are you okay?" Jace asked again.

Dodie rubbed her stomach, and felt again the wonder of this tiny being inside of her. The miracle of life that she and Jace had created together.

She looked up at her husband, the man she had pledged her life to and who had pledged his life to her.

In front of her family and friends.

"I'm fine, Jace Scholte. God is surrounding us with His care and love, and I am fine."

Jace knelt before her and smiled up at her. "Me, too." Then he laid his head on his child, safe in its mother's womb. "Us, too."

* * * * *

Dear Reader,

I've never went through what Dodie did, and I can't begin to be an expert, but I know women who have been sexually abused. Daily I admire the strength and courage of those who managed to carry on with this memory embedded in their lives. I can't claim to have any answers for healing, but I do know that our God is a loving and caring God, and that He understands pain and sorrow and shame. And that in spite of how we may view Him, His love is boundless and all-reaching. If we let Him into our lives, if we realize that apart from Him we have no good thing, then maybe we can find strength and hope and unconditional love.

Carolyne Aarsen

P.S. Stop by my Web site at www.carolyneaarsen.com, or drop me a note at caarsen@xplornet.com.

DISCUSSION QUESTIONS

1. Do you think Dodie's reaction to what happened to her was realistic?

2. Why would she feel shame when she had done nothing wrong?

3. Why do you think she kept this information from Jace and from her parents?

4. How would you have reacted in this situation?

5. Dodie used to be focused and far more conservative. Why do you think she changed so much?

6. What should Jace have done when she left the first time?

7. Why do think Dodie's mother reacted the way she did when she was finally told? Could you empathize with her?

8. If your daughter gave you this news, what would your reaction be? Or, conversely, if you had to tell your family, what do you think their reaction would be?

9. Was Dodie right in being angry with God? How would you feel toward Him if you had been in the same situation?

10. Why do you think Jace's career was so important to him? Do you think shame was part of his past, as well? Why or why not?

11. Which part of the book did you enjoy most?

12. Why do you think Dodie kept the information about what happened to her from her sister? If you have a sister, would you have?

13. Do you know someone who has experienced the same thing Dodie has? Have you been able to comfort them or talk to them?

*Here's a sneak peek at "Merry Mayhem"
by Margaret Daley,
one of the two riveting suspense stories in the
new collection CHRISTMAS PERIL,
available in December 2009
from Love Inspired Suspense.*

"Run. Disappear… Don't trust anyone, especially the police."

Annie Coleman almost dropped the phone at her ex-boyfriend's words, but she couldn't. She had to keep it together for her daughter. Jayden played nearby, oblivious to the sheer terror Annie was feeling at hearing Bryan's gasped warning.

"Thought you could get away," a gruff voice she didn't recognize said between punches. "You haven't finished telling me what I need to know."

Annie panicked. What was going on? What was happening to Bryan on the other end? Confusion gripped her in a chokehold, her chest tightening with each inhalation.

"I don't want," Bryan's rattling gasp punctuated the brief silence, "any money. Just let me go. I'll forget everything."

"I'm not worried about you telling a soul." The menace in the assailant's tone underscored his deadly intent. "All I need to know is exactly where you hid it. If you tell me now, it will be a lot less painful."

"I can't—" Agony laced each word.

"What's that? A phone?" the man screamed.

The sounds of a struggle then a gunshot blasted her eardrum. Curses roared through the connection.

Fear paralyzed Annie in the middle of her kitchen. Was Bryan shot? Dead?

The voice on the phone returned. "Who's this? Who are you?"

The assailant's voice so clear on the phone panicked her. She slammed it down onto its cradle as though that action could sever the memories from her mind. But nothing would. Had she heard her daughter's father being killed? What information did Bryan have? Did that man know her name? Question after question bombarded her from all sides, but inertia held her still.

The ringing of the phone jarred her out of her trance. Her gaze zoomed in on the lighted panel on the receiver and saw the call was from Bryan's cell. The assailant had her home telephone number. He could discover where she lived. He knew what she'd heard.

"Mommy, what's wrong?"

Looking up at Jayden, Annie schooled her features into what she hoped was a calm expression while her stomach reeled. "You know, I've been thinking, honey, we need to take a vacation. It's time for us to have an adventure. Let's see how fast you can pack." Although she tried to make it sound like a game, her voice quavered, and Annie curled her trembling hands until her fingernails dug into her palms.

At the door, her daughter paused, cocking her head. "When will we be coming back?"

The question hung in the air, and Annie wondered if they'd ever be able to come back at all.

* * * * *

*Follow Annie and Jayden as they flee to Christmas,
Oklahoma, and hide from a killer—with a little
help from a small-town police officer.*

*Look for CHRISTMAS PERIL
by Margaret Daley and Debby Giusti,
available December 2009
from Love Inspired Suspense.*

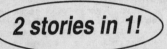

REQUEST YOUR FREE BOOKS!

2 FREE INSPIRATIONAL NOVELS
PLUS 2
FREE
MYSTERY GIFTS

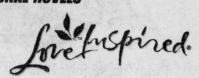

YES! Please send me 2 FREE Love Inspired® novels and my 2 FREE mystery gifts (gifts are worth about $10). After receiving them, if I don't wish to receive any more books, I can return the shipping statement marked "cancel". If I don't cancel, I will receive 4 brand-new novels every month and be billed just $4.24 per book in the U.S. or $4.74 per book in Canada. That's a savings of over 20% off the cover price. It's quite a bargain! Shipping and handling is just 50¢ per book.* I understand that accepting the 2 free books and gifts places me under no obligation to buy anything. I can always return a shipment and cancel at any time. Even if I never buy another book, the two free books and gifts are mine to keep forever.

113 IDN EYK2 313 IDN EYLE

Name	(PLEASE PRINT)

Address	Apt. #

City	State/Prov.	Zip/Postal Code

Signature (if under 18, a parent or guardian must sign)

Mail to Steeple Hill Reader Service:
IN U.S.A.: P.O. Box 1867, Buffalo, NY 14240-1867
IN CANADA: P.O. Box 609, Fort Erie, Ontario L2A 5X3

Not valid to current subscribers of Love Inspired books.

Want to try two free books from another series?
Call 1-800-873-8635 or visit www.morefreebooks.com

* Terms and prices subject to change without notice. Prices do not include applicable taxes. Sales tax applicable in N.Y. Canadian residents will be charged applicable provincial taxes and GST. Offer not valid in Quebec. This offer is limited to one order per household. All orders subject to approval. Credit or debit balances in a customer's account(s) may be offset by any other outstanding balance owed by or to the customer. Please allow 4 to 6 weeks for delivery. Offer available while quantities last.

Your Privacy: Steeple Hill Books is committed to protecting your privacy. Our Privacy Policy is available online at www.SteepleHill.com or upon request from the Reader Service. From time to time we make our lists of customers available to reputable third parties who may have a product or service of interest to you. If you would prefer we not share your name and address, please check here. ☐